CHERRINGHAM

A COSY MYSTERY SERIES

THE BODY IN THE LAKE

Neil Richards • Matthew Costello

RED DOG
UK

Cherringham is a long-running mystery series set in the Cotswolds. The stories are self-contained, though many will enjoy reading them in order of publication:

1.

GRACIOUS HOSTS

SARAH TURNED OFF the main road and pulled up at the pillared gatehouse to Repton Hall. She looked up at the stone columns: on each stood a bronze stag. The tall wrought-iron gates that stood between them and protected the Estate were closed, but as she prepared to get out and…

… do what? Ring a bell? Do places like this even have doorbells?

… they magically opened.

She glanced up at the stuccoed entrance walls. Nestled discreetly beneath one of the stags she spotted a camera. Somewhere within the Estate, she realised, a security guard was watching her on a monitor.

Clearly her tatty old Rav-4 had passed the test — and now she understood why Simon Repton's secretary had asked for her registration number.

As she drove through the gates, past the tasteful steel sign — 'Repton Hall: Country House and Conference Centre' — she remembered how, only a couple of years ago, there had been rumours that the Repton family, house and all, were heading for bankruptcy.

This was quite the turnaround.

From the looks of it, the long driveway had recently been re-laid, and as she travelled along it towards the imposing Queen Anne mansion which glowed in the afternoon sunshine, she could see they'd also spent a fortune on the gardens.

The trees were shaped and pruned; the rolling meadows trim; fences freshly painted — and to one side of the house the famous ornamental lake sparkled.

Last time she'd been here — to a rather sad agricultural show two summers ago — the lake had been stagnant and green. But now its waters were clear and on the little island at its centre, the Georgian folly — a classical temple — stood proud again.

Sarah smiled to herself. In part she and Jack must have been responsible for this miraculous turn-around. Some time ago they'd solved the mystery of a missing Roman artefact on Repton land — the successful case had benefited the redoubtable Lady Repton to the tune of half a million, so the rumours went.

But now as she drove past the side of the house towards the 'conference car park' she guessed that the Reptons must have picked up at least another million elsewhere to complete this transformation.

For, behind the graceful mansion, a low brick-and-timber extension had been added, with cool clear lines that suggested the work of an expensive architect.

This was the conference centre — where in a couple of hours she was going to deliver her little performance...

The car park was nearly full but she found a space, grabbed her MacAir, locked up, and headed to the side entrance.

"Hey, nice timing," said a voice behind her.

She turned to see Simon Repton himself walking round the side of the house. Lean, tanned, in a charcoal hand-made suit, Simon exuded money, confidence, charm, and success.

At least that's what he thinks, thought Sarah.

Slimy Simey — that's what her assistant Grace had called him, and Sarah had to work hard not to say the name to his face.

"Simon," she said. "How lovely to see you again."

Simon approached and gave her a kiss on each cheek, lingering just a little longer than was quite necessary.

"We're still at the champers stage, so you've got plenty of time to set up."

"Everything going okay?"

"*Absolument parfait!*" he said with a faux-Gallic shrug, his boyish fringe swinging across his eyes. "Our guests are having a *tres bonne temps!*"

"How wonderful that you speak French," said Sarah, guessing that she should acknowledge the performance.

"One of the benefits of an awfully expensive education, Sarah," he said. "Though to be honest, I do believe the esteemed delegation representing St. Martin sur Mer has a better grasp of English than most of our staff."

"That's good, because the presentation's going to be entirely in English — some of it Cherringham English too."

"I'm sure you'll make it clear as day, babes."

Slimy Simey indeed.

"And I wouldn't worry over-much," he continued. "I'm told we're a shoo-in. Your little PowerPoint's just the icing on the cake."

"Terrific," said Sarah, thinking about the hours that she and Grace had slaved over it, hoping it was worth more than just the *icing.*

"Not that we can do without it, of course," Simon said hastily, obviously spotting the dismay on Sarah's face, "After all, it's the official reason they've flown over here to see us!"

Sarah was impressed with his quick recovery.

"Why don't I show you to the media room and you can get yourself all Wi-Fi'd and ready to go?"

He put an arm around her shoulder and steered her towards a door in the new block. She pulled away a few inches, letting the unwanted limb dangle in the air before falling.

"I think, by the way, you'll find the whole thing pretty damned state of the art," he said. "Cost Granny a fortune!"

They entered the building and Sarah could see the long corridor that led back to the main house — impeccably decorated, with cedar floors, soft-toned wood panelling, and fabric walls.

On one side of the corridor was a line of oil portraits of grim-faced Reptons past and present. On the other, framed black-and-white photos showed armies of house staff, standing to attention on the steps of the house.

"Family tradition," said Simon as Sarah leaned in to examine one of the photos. "Every Boxing Day for a hundred years the grateful Estate workers grabbed their bonus and lined up for the team photo."

"Quite a collection," said Sarah.

"Daddy's archive," said Simon. "I've been digitising it. Yanks love it."

Then, with a tap to her shoulder, Simon steered her the other way towards the 'media room'.

"Lots of break-out areas for brainstorming," he said on the way, pointing out rooms off to the side, each filled with sofas, cushions, and low tables. "And through here we've got the leisure centre."

"Very impressive," said Sarah.

"Isn't it? Pool and gym aren't open yet, but the hot tub, steam rooms and sauna block is up and running. Hope you'll join us after dinner for a little fun?"

"Ah," she said quickly. "You know how it is — working mum — got to be home by midnight."

Simon looked disappointed.

"Pumpkin time, huh?" he said. "Shame. I was hoping you'd stay over. Anyway—"

Dream on, she thought.

He stopped by one door and opened it to reveal a small lecture theatre with cinema style seats, a screen and a presentation area.

"And here's the media room. Get yourself sorted — and I'll bring the mob through in an hour."

With that, Sarah watched him turn and go — as if he'd suddenly realised there was more fun to be had elsewhere.

"Toodle pip!" he said as he left.

The door swung shut and Sarah looked around the room.

Could be a West End screening room, she thought, taking her laptop and setting it down on a table at the front.

Let's hope they like what I'm going to show them…

SARAH MOVED IN a way she hoped looked confident across the

stage in front of the presentation screen and clicked for the next slide.

Public presentations weren't really her forte, but this seemed to be going well. All eyes were on her, and despite the amount of champagne consumed, the audience appeared to be totally with her.

"So, here in Cherringham we hope you agree that the business case is clear. The social value. The cultural importance. Our two villages are the perfect fit — St. Martin and Cherringham — both deeply proud of their long history, confident of a long future. Friendly, outward-looking, hospitable. Have there ever been two better candidates for twinning?"

Even in the low light of the room, Sarah could see smiling faces, nodding heads.

And she knew it wasn't just the effect of the stream of hors d'oeuvres and bubbly which Simon's army of waiters had been pouring for the last hour.

"Finally — who better to join in what I hope will be a happy occasion — the children of Cherringham themselves…"

Stepping to one side, she clicked play on the last video and took a deep breath of relief.

Up on the screen the kids of Cherringham Primary sang their hearts out in a raucous, affectionate 'open letter' to the mayor and deputy mayor of St. Martin, telling them they should "do it for the kids" and sign that agreement "Toot Sweet!"

She scanned the audience. There were plenty of faces she recognised — the great and the good of Cherringham. Tony Standish — her old friend and family solicitor; Cecil Cauldwell, local property bigwig; Harry Howden — no-nonsense owner of Howdens Holdings, one of the biggest agri-businesses in the area; June Rigby, chair of the parish council; Lee Jones, vice-chair. There were several other familiar faces from the village — but not people she could actually name.

All were gathered here for a weekend of wine and fine dining to persuade the mercurial French delegation to finally agree to a twinning arrangement — a proposition to become "sister" villages — which had been in the works for over a year.

She looked at the two visitors from St. Martin — the mayor and his deputy.

Laurent Bourdin — built like a bull — though one aged by a lifetime of brandy and Gauloises, she guessed.

And Marie Duval — slight, elegant, aloof, and beautiful.

They were smiling. Good sign? Perhaps. By all accounts, they were proving tough nuts to crack.

Sarah hoped that her contribution might just make up their minds at last.

On a final crashing chord the house lights went up and Sarah was thrilled to see her little audience rise to their feet laughing and applauding.

Simon came over from the side, clapping her.

"Ladies and gentlemen, Madame et Monsieur *le maire* — our very own Sarah Edwards, giving you the real human reason why we all hope you'll give your blessing this weekend to our historic and ambitious twinning proposal!"

The good-natured applause continued.

"Now, if you'd all make your way to the Queen Mary room — dinner is about to be served!"

Sarah waited while Simon ushered the crowd away. At the door he turned back to her:

"Totally fab, Sarah — not a wrong note. Awesome."

"Thanks, Simon."

"Now come on — let's get them drunk, give 'em a pen and force the Frenchies to sign!"

Sarah couldn't fault his enthusiasm. Whether he was in it for himself, the Reptons or the village — Simon certainly gave his all for the cause.

2.

ENTENTE CORDIALE

"LEAVE THE EU? No way, Laurent! There's still a few bob to be made, ain't that right, Harry?"

Lee Jones, vice-chair of Cherringham Council and owner of a local luxury 4WD franchise, grinned at Harry Howden then turned to Sarah sitting next to him and winked.

"Harry won't be happy until his Turkey-Pops are filling every freezer in Europe," Lee continued.

Across the dining table Laurent Bourdin raised his glass to Lee: "Just as long as I don't have to eat them, Messieurs…"

"I have to say I'm with you on that one, Monsieur Bourdin," said Tony from further down the table. "No offence intended, Harry old chap."

"None taken," said Harry Howden raising his glass with what looked to Sarah like a very weary smile. "But I don't see the problem with exporting a little modern food-industry know-how to our friends in St. Martin—"

"We welcome it," said Marie Duval.

Sarah turned to see the French deputy mayor smiling graciously — and looking directly not at Harry Howden, but at Lee.

"And in return perhaps we can introduce you to some of the more sophisticated pleasures of French culture."

"Looking forward to it already," said Lee raising his glass back at her.

"Would that be before or after the cricket match?" said a voice from the far end of the table.

Everyone already pretty lubricated, Sarah could tell.

Relaxed. Joking.

For now...

"No, I forbid it!" said Laurent banging his hand down on the table in mock outrage. "There will be no cricket in St. Martin — *non!*"

"Put that in the contract, Tony!" shouted Simon from the head of the table.

"Not another bloody clause!" came a voice from somewhere.

"Anything Brussels can do, we can do better—"

"Throw another crate of this red in and I'll sign anything," said Lee. "Amazing!"

Sarah joined in the laughter and hardly noticed her glass being filled.

But it was too late to say no to more wine.

Somewhere between the fish, the sorbet, and the meat courses, Sarah had given up her promise to herself that she wouldn't drink. The quality stuff was on offer tonight. How could she refuse?

Yes — she had to be up early to take Daniel to football, yes — she had a week's housework to do, yes — she'd promised to go through Chloe's essay on Anthony and Cleopatra... A busy Sunday ahead!

But she'd quickly realised that the meal — and the drinking — was going to go on for ever and the only way to get through it was to just go with the flow.

And was the wine ever flowing now.

There were twenty places at the dining table, and Simon had spared no expense. The candelabra were lit, the silver shone, the crystal sparkled, and the food was exquisite, even by French standards.

But now — three hours into the event — all pretence at formality had long gone and tongues were not only loosened, they were positively flapping.

She sat back and scanned the room. Part of her job was to write up this historic dinner as part of the official press release — and then in a week's time take pictures of the actual signing of the Twinning Agreement.

If it wasn't all going to end up as a blur she needed to take notes now. In truth though, it was hardly what she'd call work. The dinner had revealed all kinds of intriguing behaviour — plenty for her and Grace to chat and laugh about on Monday...

The mayor and deputy mayor from St. Martin for instance.

They weren't married — at least not to each other. But by all accounts they were a couple — Simon had whispered to her that they had requested a double room.

An odd couple at that: Laurent was in his sixties, blustering, red-faced, the bulging body of an ex-rugby player. And Marie: much younger, was rail thin, the archetypal political mistress; alluring on the outside and tough as nails inside, Sarah had no doubt.

And yet... Was there a hint of something here also going on between Marie and Lee?

There'd been half a dozen 'exploratory' trips to France over the last couple of years and from what she'd heard, Lee was just the kind of chap to take that kind of exploring literally.

Just before they'd all taken their seats Sarah had noticed the Cherringham vice-chair whispering briefly in Marie's pretty little ear...

Then there was Harry Howden — gruff, no-nonsense Harry.

Rumour had it he was aiming to snap up some prime French property on the back of this partnership and build himself a meat processing plant in St. Martin.

Won't the locals love that.

Next to Harry, Cecil Cauldwell helped himself to another glass of wine. This event was right up his street, Sarah could tell. Eating, drinking, and smooth-talking potential customers — he was in his element. And why not? The proposed twinning arrangement would give an extra spur to the little French property business he had started up, expanding from the Cotswolds to the sunny south of France.

Raucous laughter burst from the far end of the table, apparently generated by Simon, their host. Was that a turkey impersonation he was doing, complete with gobbling noises?

People were weeping with laughter.

And what was in it for Simon? Surely Cherringham Council wasn't picking up the bill for this junket? She'd seen that he had his eye on Marie — perhaps he imagined a never-ending line of French fillies queuing up to use the Repton Hall spa?

She looked to the other end of the table, where June Rigby was deep in conversation with Harry Howden's wife, Vanessa.

June was quiet and demure, but she was active on the council and had big political ambitions, or so Sarah had heard. Was she looking for a role at Westminster one day? And if so, perhaps Simon and the Repton name might be able to help?

She spotted them exchanging looks. Perhaps he'd given up hope of a French partner tonight and was going to settle for the prim English maid?

And what of Harry's grim-faced wife, Vanessa? How would the twinning affect her? Vanessa was a self-proclaimed moral authority in the village — frequently writing to the local paper about the out of control "yoof", the over-liberal licensing hours, the decline in social standards. Would her turkey-farmer husband be able to resist the dubious temptations of a French sea-side resort?

Ooh, this is too much fun, thought Sarah.

At which point the chairs at the far end of the table were kicked back, music blared, and Sarah saw that a conga line had formed with Simon at its head.

As the surprised waiting staff retreated to the edges of the room, the conga line laughed and stumbled its way around the table. "La la la la la la! La la la la la la!" they all began singing.

The line picked up more dancers as it went — and Sarah watched as it disappeared out of the room.

Waiter, cheque please, she thought.

Time to go.

Sarah looked around the table at the half dozen remaining guests. June looked embarrassed. Harry Howden was grinning —

but Vanessa looked disgusted, her lips pursed. Tony Standish, as always, seemed remarkably tolerant.

Laurent and Marie were blinking in astonishment.

The conga line could be heard going up and down the corridors outside.

"La la la la la la! La la la la la la!"

In the Queen Anne room, the remaining diners sat totally quiet. Suddenly, it was all too awkward.

"*Les Anglais,*" said Sarah smiling apologetically, trying to break the silence. "They'll be back, I'm sure."

And noisily they soon were.

"Come on you spoilsports!" cried Simon as the conga line burst into the room and swayed past the seated guests.

Simon whisked June Rigby up from her seat to join in. There was a quick exchange in French between June and Laurent as she passed him, stony-faced. Sarah could only assume it was an apology for the behaviour of her English colleagues…

Sarah watched as Cherringham's Council chief awkwardly led the dancing line.

Round and round the table the line stumbled.

"La la la la la la! La la la la la la!"

"More champagne!" cried Simon.

"Champagne! Champagne!" echoed those behind Simon.

"La la la la la la! La la la la la la!"

Sarah looked at her watch. Still only eleven o'clock. She wondered where this evening would end…

And maybe — now — how…

SARAH STUMBLED INTO the fresh air at one in the morning. Standing outside on the gravel in front of the beautiful old house, it was hard to believe that the party was still going on within.

But it was…

Those party games.

Had they really played Sardines?

Had she really hidden in a cupboard with a French mayor while her own solicitor tiptoed around the room whispering 'come out, come out, wherever you are'?

She shook her head in horror.

Luckily she was the one responsible for writing up the report of the evening for the parish council — and she knew exactly which parts would be censored.

Slowly the more sensible guests had drifted home, but there was still a hard-core party group remaining in the house. She'd sneaked away to get her coat from the ever-patient cloakroom staff, and managed to escape the house without being noticed.

Or so she thought.

Simon appeared at the doorway.

"Don't go. Can't go *now*," he'd said. "Now's when the fun starts."

He came over and swayed boozily next to her.

"That's what's worrying me," said Sarah, just keeping her balance herself.

"Hot tub's filling up," he said. "Dress code's *au naturel* or so I hear. Everyone's feeling jolly frisky…"

"I'm sure they are," said Sarah. "Oh look — there's my taxi!"

A set of headlights swung round into the drive in front of them both.

Thank God, she thought.

"Kissee kissee goodnight at least," said Simon, his face drifting closer to hers, eyes shut…

But Sarah disappeared.

Nick of time, she thought.

3.

THE ISLAND ON THE LAKE

LAURENT STOOD AT the edge of the lake, took a deep drag of his cigarette, and peered into the darkness.

The lake stretched ahead, the water flat and black in the moonless night. He could just make out the shape of the island and the little Greek temple which stood upon it.

A folly, they called it.

Folly.

Bien sur. So very… English!

This whole project was a folly and he wanted to wash his hands of it.

Nothing good had come from it and nothing good ever would. *Rien!*

These people with their grand ideas and their patronising views. Getting drunk on such good wine! And never following through with the money. Always "a little cash-flow problem".

He shivered.

Should have put a jacket on.

Not in the south of France now.

Mon Dieu — I wish I was home.

But he couldn't go home — yet. He had work to do. One final meeting. Why on the island though? It didn't make sense.

He'd left the hot tub when things got too wild. Then Simon Repton had cornered him in the empty bar. Making all sorts of promises. Slurring his words… *"You'll do the deal, hmm?"*

Laurent didn't like being cornered, so that meeting hadn't gone quite as expected.

But what did he care? Rich bastard needed bringing down a little.

He'd wandered around the place looking for Marie but he couldn't find her. Then he'd gone back to his room to lie down — and found the note under the door.

Someone telling him they had to meet — now.

So here he was out in the cold night looking for a way to get out to the damn island.

So very… *caché*!

He thought back to when they'd arrived that the morning and Simon and his grandmother had given them a tour of the Estate. There had been some boats, he was sure of it.

He wandered along the edge of the lake, slipping on the wet grass.

Ah-ha — there they were.

Two small rowing-boats were tied to a metal stake set into the bank.

He held one steady and clambered in, half-falling.

Was he still drunk? Maybe, a little.

There were two oars — and rowlocks.

Good.

Untying the rope, he used one of the oars to push off, then spun the little boat round, sat, and began to row towards the island.

Fifty years living by the sea, he knew how to row.

He felt the oars dig deep in the black water and the boat slide smoothly. Ahead of him he could see the outline of Repton Hall. Some windows were still lit.

In one upper room a figure appeared at a window, silhouetted.

Could they see him?

It was unlikely — so dark out here on the lake.

The figure disappeared.

To bed? Or was the party still going on? Surely not, it was nearly three in the morning.

Incroyable…

He looked over his shoulder.

The island was now just a few metres away and he could clearly see the temple.

There was a faint glow from within — a light on?

He shipped the oars and the boat glided on, bumping against rocks until it reached the grassy bank of the island.

He climbed out carefully and tied the rope to a tree stump.

Then he stood up on the rough grass, looked around and listened.

Not a sound.

And no other boats, as far as he could tell.

What was this — some kind of trick? Another stupid English joke.

But no — there was a sound now, a faint sound from inside the temple.

Laurent shivered again.

And suddenly felt a sliver of fear. The hairs on his arm were standing up.

What am I afraid of? he thought, surprised at his own emotions.

No — it must be the cold. The chilly night air out here on the lake.

He walked up the sloping grass towards the temple, his eyes now adjusting to the darkness.

He faced tall marble pillars and just behind them, a large metal door which must open on to the temple interior. The door — not quite shut.

And inside — yes, he was right — there was some kind of light.

Quietly he approached the door, and reached out to nudge it.

He sniffed the air. There was a scent — familiar…

He pushed the door hard and it swung open.

The inside was lit by candles — small tea-lights — it seemed like hundreds of them, like stars. And on the floor were cushions and blankets.

And there, ahead of him, he saw someone standing in the shadows.

Not waiting for him, but startled.

He took another step closer and finally — in the scant light —

he could see who it was, but not understanding, now suddenly confused.

And all Laurent Bourdin could do was say *"Non."*

4.

THE MORNING AFTER

JACK PUSHED OPEN the door to his boat, the Grey Goose, and the morning sunlight hit him square in the face. A slight breeze blew, carrying the scent of the grassy field only steps away. Looking down to the water, the Thames lapped gently by the side of the boat.

The dream, he thought.

He and Katherine had planned to come and retire here. Have this crazy kind of life; an English life for two Americans.

What fun it would be, they both agreed.

And then — as if the whole thing was a joke, the dream simply that — Katherine got sick, and began slipping away bit by bit, day by day.

Until she was gone. And for some reason, Jack had decided to come here anyway. He knew she would have wanted that.

Yes, to stand here, on a picture-perfect morning in the Cotswolds. Katherine would have loved it.

He heard the kettle whistling behind him. Riley came up and nuzzled him, ready for his walk.

"Yes," Jack said to his Springer. "Let's get this day going."

HE WALKED ON the mushy field, dodging places where the tufts of grass gave way to oozing piles of mud.

Riley seemed to have learned how to navigate the field, barely getting any dirt on his legs as he dashed away from Jack, then ran back as if fetching an imaginary ball.

Jack walked with a tall mug of English Breakfast tea, the warmth in his hands wonderful. This was not his world, but Jack loved it anyway.

The dog raced up to Jack as if he should begin running with him. Back in the day, Jack had loved a nice long run. Especially after a long tour on the streets. Cleared the head.

His wobbly knees ended that.

Riley cocked his head, barked, and then streamed away, running fast, zig-zagging in the direction of the ancient church that sat on the western end of the field where a small road passed by.

Jack started following Riley's path, sipping the already cooling tea, when he felt his phone vibrate.

He slid the phone out of his jacket pocket, already guessing who was calling.

"Jack, Sarah here."

"Good morning, Sarah," he said.

"Jack, I'm at Tony's office. He gave me a call."

"Tell Tony 'hi'," Jack said. Riley had reached the end of his invisible tether and started racing back.

Jack liked Tony Standish, the very epitome of a British solicitor and, for Sarah and her parents, a trusted family advisor.

But Jack waited. He guessed that if Sarah was calling him, there would be a reason.

"Can you pop over here, do you think?"

Her voice, a mix of strained and excited.

"Let me guess," Jack said. "Something's happened?"

Cherringham may be a small village, but people were people everywhere, from the streets of New York to the village lanes here.

"Yes."

He waited, thinking she would add some detail about her call, her request to come.

Then: "Best I tell you when you get here. I need your help, Jack."

And without knowing what the call was about, what Tony had

contacted Sarah for, Jack nodded as if they were standing there, in the field.

"Sure. Let me get Riley back on the Goose and I'll run right over."

Then — again, maybe with a good friend's sense of something in the air — Sarah said, "Thanks."

And Jack, his day begun, said, "No problem. See you soon."

On a perfect, blue-sky day, one his wife would have loved, Jack was curious about what lay ahead.

"COFFEE, JACK?"

"Most definitely, black will be fine." The solicitor's secretary stood at the door and nodded to Jack. "Right away, Mr. Brennan."

Mr. Brennan.

Jack felt like a homeless person standing in the impeccable office. Tony dressed — as usual — in a crisp dark suit, maroon tie, with a neatly folded handkerchief protruding from his breast pocket.

Jack, on the other hand, still wore the rumpled jeans he had slipped into that morning, a flannel shirt that — for all Jack knew — was dotted with last night's dinner. His black shoes were spotty from the morning's walk; mud now dried to a light brown.

He did say he'd run right over...

Jack took a chair and Tony's receptionist, a prim, grey haired woman, quietly brought the cup of coffee.

"Thank you, Emma." Tony smiled and waited until the door was shut.

"So what's up?" Jack said.

Tony turned to Sarah. "Sarah, would you like to tell Jack what this is all about? Terrible business, I'm afraid. Not good at all."

Jack sipped the dark rich coffee. He turned to Sarah.

"It's about last night, Jack. At Lady Repton's..."

And she began.

"In the lake, they found a body."

Jack nodded, sat back, and listened.

A body in the lake.
She certainly had his attention.

5.

THE BODY

SARAH STARTED BY describing the previous night's event to Jack — the big bash to woo the French mayor and his deputy for a twinning arrangement.

She had to explain that term. *Twinning*. Seemed like in the States they called it a 'sister town'.

Two countries separated by a common language.

How true.

She explained her role and the PowerPoint presentation she'd given: Cherringham and St. Martin, connected, the opportunities for both.

Then, the dinner, the drinking, the — *God, she was embarrassed to say it* — conga line.

"You didn't, um, do that?" Jack said with a small smile.

Sarah shook her head.

"No, but everyone was well beyond tipsy. It was nearly one by the time I left. Probably should have gone earlier. But it did seem to be spinning out of control."

Now Tony jumped in to carry on.

"I must confess; I only stayed a little longer. After all, I was the solicitor of record for the arrangement."

"And Tony I don't imagine you… conga-ed?"

Tony took the question in earnest.

"Heavens no. I was a mere spectator to them all, laughing, drinking. When the party continued in the hot tub, I made my excuses and left."

"Oh, dear," Jack said. "Doesn't sound very Cherringham."

"*Exactly.*"

"Tony called me this morning," Sarah said.

"Indeed," the solicitor continued. "The police have been all over the place, talking to everyone. It's becoming something of an international scandal at this point."

"The body?" Jack said.

"Laurent Bourdin, mayor of St. Martin. It appears he was so drunk he took the little rowing boat, went over to the folly—"

"Folly?"

Jack turned to Sarah.

"Oh — it's, well, like a temple, something Grecian. Just decorative, really. Built on a small island in the centre of the lake."

"Sounds aptly named."

"It seems he got as far as the island," Tony went on, "then he must have slipped on the mud, fallen back in the water and smacked his head on a boulder."

"Nasty. So the body…?"

"Just floated on the lake. Until this morning. Lady Repton spotted it first. Called the police — as you say — *asap.*"

Jack nodded.

And Sarah knew he was thinking. Putting all the details together.

Those New York detective instincts, honed on the mean streets of Manhattan. "Sarah and I can tell you about who was there. Quite a large crowd. The local great and the good."

Still, Jack hadn't said anything.

But then…

He looked at Sarah, then to Tony, brow furrowed.

"The drunken mayor slipped, knocked himself out, drowned. Police on it." He took a breath. "So why call Sarah, or me?"

Tony sniffed the air.

"It's Lady Repton, Jack. You know her, of course."

"Do indeed. Great old lady."

"Well, all this — it's terribly embarrassing. And the event, spearheaded by her grandson—"

Tony hesitated. Jack could tell that Simon Repton was not Tony's cup of tea. "Simon Repton. Has big plans for the old place. Now she's worried about the family name."

"But the police *are* involved, yes?"

"Of course. Alan is over there this morning. CID from Oxford due shortly, I've heard. Looks like an accident. But still, well, as I said, you know Lady Repton."

Sarah had her eyes on Jack. Maybe he was right. Nothing more than an accident for the police to investigate.

He looked over then, as if sensing her eyes on him. "Okay. I guess we could talk to her."

"And Simon," Tony added. "It was his 'show' last night, so to speak. The manor house turned into a conference centre. His dream, using his grandmother's money to be sure."

Tony looked from Jack then to Sarah. "Would you? It would be a great favour. Just a terrible accident, I'm sure."

"I'm sure,' Jack said.

Does he mean that? Sarah thought.

Jack stood up, and extended a hand to the solicitor.

And Sarah felt that maybe there were things Jack hadn't said that she would soon hear once they stepped outside.

"SO JACK, WHAT do you think?"

For a moment he didn't look at her, squinting in the sunlight.

He turned to her. "You know, Sarah, sometimes an accident is just that: an accident."

He shook his head.

"I know, but it wouldn't hurt for us — to look into it. If only to pacify Lady Repton."

Jack nodded. Then: "It's police business. They have their team, on it. I dunno, Sarah…"

Sarah kept her response short, to the point.

"Yes. But what if we can help?"

Then one added fact.

"And we *have* helped people."

Jack nodded again. Took a deep breath. The truth of that clear. Case closed.

And then — he smiled. "Sure."

Said with all the warmth that she had grown to like so much.

"Wouldn't hurt for us to ask a few questions. Be interesting to meet this Simon fellow."

"I doubt very much you'll like him," Sarah said.

Jack laughed.

"I gathered that from Tony's take on him."

"The man's an octopus — if you know what I mean," Sarah said, triggering another laugh from Jack.

Jack looked around again.

"And not a bad day weather-wise," he said. "The Sprite, top down?"

"Brilliant," Sarah said, following him to the small sports car he'd parked by the Village Hall, the minuscule vehicle with its tall driver already a familiar sight in the village.

And they drove to Repton Hall, in silence, enjoying the light, the wind and this rather spectacular day.

6.

SIMON

PULLING INTO THE gravel roundabout in front of the grand Georgian house, Jack saw a police car.

"Looks like Alan's still here."

Jack was never certain how Alan would respond to them. With their help, mysteries had certainly been solved. These days, Alan seemed not to mind them getting involved — at least not as much as he did when Jack and Sarah first started their little "investigations".

A good solid beat cop, Jack would have called him back in NYC. Perfect for a sleepy village like Cherringham.

It was only when things got complicated could he be over his head.

Alan popped out of his car as Jack pulled up.

"And it looks like he's expecting us," Jack said.

Sarah nodded. Jack knew that she had history with the officer, which made things complicated for her.

Jack parked the Sprite, and then he and Sarah got out of the car.

Alan's face was set, serious.

"Morning, Alan," Jack said.

A nod. "Lady Repton said she had asked to see you two. Thought I'd wait. It's very much a police matter here, you know."

"I'm sure," Jack said.

"Alan, we just were going to talk to Lady Repton and Simon,"

Sarah said. "She's worried about the incident, the publicity."

The officer nodded, then pointed to the water's edge. "Just make sure you don't go anywhere down there. We've got yellow tape over by the trees. But the whole lake is off-limits. Least till the SOCO gets here."

"Absolutely," Jack said. "Just here to talk." He fired a glance at Sarah.

"Right, and maybe reassure Lady Repton," she added.

"Okay. Yes—" Alan took his time. "Guess that's okay."

Not that he could stop us, Jack thought. Still, better to keep on Alan's good side.

"Alan," said Sarah. "Just curious — can we ask you a bit about the body, where they found it?"

"Bobbing out there, on the lake. Looks like whatever nonsense went on here last night, the mayor from St. Martin took it into his head to row out to the island. What was he thinking? Slipped, and fractured his skull."

Jack nodded. "He didn't drown?"

"HE WAS FLOATING face down. Not my area of expertise, Jack. That will require a post-mortem. But the hole in his skull looked lethal enough to kill him."

Alan's radio squawked, and he turned back to his patrol car. "She's inside. And that grandson of hers too."

Another Simon fan, Jack thought.

"Thanks," Sarah said, and Jack followed her up the steps and into the house.

"IT'S ALL COMING back to me," Sarah said. "Last night, here, way too much wine."

Jack looked around. Though the place was opulent, he could see signs of things beginning to slip. A bit of frayed carpet, the wood railing of the staircase not as gleaming and shiny as it should be.

They were standing in what he guessed was a classic sitting

room. White antimacassars covered the arms and headrests of claw-footed easy chairs.

Just like Grandma's place in Brooklyn Heights, Jack thought. A room out of a museum collection.

He turned to Sarah. "So, the plan was for this place to become a modern conference centre?"

Sarah nodded. "There's a big new extension at the back with meeting rooms and a leisure centre. And they'll use the dining room in the main building of course. But I can't imagine this room will be part of the 'package'."

A sudden clearing of a throat signalled that they weren't alone.

And Jack turned to see Lady Repton, standing next to a lanky man.

Simon.

Jack looked at him. Simon's eyes were shifting everywhere except landing on Jack.

There is a guy who looks like he may have a secret or two, he thought.

SARAH STIRRED HER teacup, making a whirlpool in the delicate china cup, sending a single sugar cup spinning. No other sweetener on offer, so the cube was it.

She and Lady Repton had brought Jack up to speed on the purpose of the event last night, the planned twinning, the local luminaries who attended.

And Lady Repton didn't hide the fact that she wasn't thrilled with her grandson's plans to turn the ancestral home into a modern conference centre. A good deal of head shaking and eye rolling accompanied her description of those "plans" and Simon's ambitions.

Simon. So quiet.

"And the cost? So much money!" she said.

Sarah waited for Simon to defend his plans, but he was much less gregarious now than he had been the night before. Not enough sleep, and probably a crashing hangover. His blood-shot eyes looked like road map.

Jack nodded. Then he pressed the point: "Simon, you were the organiser of the event?"

Finally, as if waiting for a bullet that would inevitably hit, Simon looked at Jack, then Sarah.

He cleared his throat. "I, er, um, provided and prepared the venue."

He parsed his words so carefully.

"The reception, though, was run by the Parish Council, of course. June Rigby, Lee Jones."

Jack looked to Sarah.

"The chair and vice-chair of the Council, Jack."

Simon nodded. "I merely provided the resources, the tech set-up for Sarah and her PowerPoint. Organised the dinner."

"And the wine?" Jack said.

That stopped Simon. The wine would be a key player in this, Sarah knew. For that accident to happen, for Laurent to stumble and smash his head on a rock… well, that would call for an *enormous* amount of wine.

Simon rubbed his nose.

"Y-yes. Though, June and Lee signed off on it all."

Jack nodded, a small smile. Sarah knew *that* smile. Disarming, one of Jack's tools of the trade.

"And you just kept it flowing?"

A nod. Then Sarah leaned close.

"Simon, after I left, I'm wondering… did anything happen that concerned you? I know you turned on the hot tub and the party went on late. Did you see the mayor leave?"

Too many questions she knew.

Lady Repton filled the gap.

"Hot tub. Spare me the details please."

Then she stood up. "I think I shall let you three chat. I don't think my constitution can handle any more discussion of that… hot tub. I shall be in the garden."

"Sure," Jack said.

Then Lady Repton paused in her flight. "And thank you both for coming."

"Glad to help," Sarah said, as the venerable lady fled the room just as some seamy details seemed about to bubble to the surface.

"YES, EVERYONE SEEMED up for it. I mean, not Tony, of course. Still—" Simon caught himself. "Or Cecil either. But Laurent got a bit worked up. I mean, everyone was—"

"Naked?" Jack said.

"Lot of wine," Simon offered. "And the mayor suddenly got upset. He'd barely plopped in — he was very large — before he stormed away."

"Upset?" Sarah said. "What about?"

"Well, lots of laughs going on between Lee and the deputy mayor. Maybe Laurent didn't appreciate that. I did go and look for him."

Jack looked over at Sarah. She imagined he had a question at the ready but in such a subtle way he was telling her to carry on.

"You were worried?" she said.

"About the mayor — no. But about the deal? Yes! It's not just a big deal for the village, you know. Big deal for this place too, the Repton Conference Centre."

"So you tried to see if Laurent was all right?"

Simon nodded. "Found him in the bar. And he was anything *but*, threatened to pull the bloody plug on everything and—"

Simon stopped, catching himself.

He rubbed his nose again, sniffed.

Maybe more than wine being liberally consumed last night, thought Sarah.

"That's it. I went to bed. Then, this morning, the police came."

"Lady Repton spotted the body?" Jack said.

Simon's head seem to sink lower.

"Yes. She wasn't sure what it was at first. Then—"

Sarah looked at Jack.

Just the kind of thing to make him angry. The old lady having to experience that.

Jack remained steady. "And that's all you know?"

A quick nod from Simon. And Sarah guessed that her friend didn't buy that at all.

Jack stood up. "Beautiful place your grandmother has here, Simon. Be a shame to have anything... anything at all endanger that, yes? Guess we all need wait on what the SOCO finds out, hmm?"

A small smile.

"Yes," Simon said, his voice hollow.

"Meanwhile, I assume it's all right for Sarah and I to talk to the other revellers? Wouldn't want any surprises to hurt your grandmother or the family name."

Another nod from Simon, as Jack walked out of the sitting room and Sarah came beside him.

"This house needs some work. But what a place."

WHEN THEY LEFT the manor house, Alan was down by the shore with a man in a SOCO white suit.

"Jack, what do you think?"

"Lots. Fancy a little ride?"

"Sure. As long as I get to hear your thoughts on all this."

He shook his head, grinning.

Jack was finally *back*.

"Oh, you will."

7.

THE SECOND BOAT

SARAH GOT OUT of Jack's Sprite, and looked around. From Repton Hall they'd driven across the main road and then climbed sharply so they were now up on top of the wooded line of hills that bordered the Repton Estate.

"You're beginning to know your way around pretty well, Jack," said Sarah. "I've never even been up here."

"Nice place to come and hike. Been doing it for a while now."

Now, as she looked around, she saw that it was indeed a beautiful spot.

"So, we here for a picnic?"

"You know — I forgot to order us a basket. But come this way…"

Jack took a path that led from the single-lane road, past the dense trees, until they reached an opening.

Sarah came beside him. The hill ended in an abrupt drop, rocky. And it gave a view across a meadow below, then the lake.

"Lady Repton's Estate," she said.

"Right. See the island?"

Down below in the valley, she could see the man in the white suit on the shore. Yellow tape fluttered around trees girding a small jetty where a rowing boat was tied up. The Scenes of Crime Officer and Alan were leaning over, looking at the boat.

"Looks from up here like they've found something," Sarah said.

"Could be. I just wanted to see the whole thing. The island, the lake, the house." He turned to her. "This is all, well, confusing."

"What do you mean?

"What would make the mayor, wobbly as he was, get into one of the rowboats and go over to that island?"

"I know. I assumed when I left that everyone was pretty close to passing out."

"You saw Simon just now? Rubbing his nose. Could be everyone had a bit of Colombian Marching Powder after you left."

"Coke?"

"I'm guessing Simon certainly did. Maybe some of the others." Jack turned and looked at her. "You know these people. That possible? Upstanding council members, sharing a line or two?"

"I wouldn't have thought so, Jack. But then — I've been at some parties where you'd be surprised who indulged."

"Right. Bit of a different attitude towards that stuff here in England, hmm?"

"Maybe — in London. But it's still a Class A drug."

"So the party went on. Hot tub fun, and Laurent ends up going to the island. Somehow he slips on those rocks and—"

Jack stopped.

"What is it?"

Sarah had grown to relish these moments when he stopped thinking aloud, when his eyes narrowed as if he was seeing puzzle pieces fall into place.

He turned to Sarah.

"Alan said that when they pulled the body out, it was face down, yes?"

"Right."

"And Laurent had fallen and smashed his head open."

"Where you taking this, Jack?"

A smile. As if explaining the basics of gravity. "Y'know I've helped pull many a body out of the water. The East River is such a convenient dumping ground. And look down there, at the island, the rocks, you have to think if he stumbled…"

She got where he was going.

Of course.

"He would have fallen *forward*. Not back."

"Not impossible, to fall backwards — but it's hard to imagine."

Then Sarah got the implications of what she and Jack were talking about. Suddenly the sunlit hill, this rocky ridge, didn't feel so warm and inviting.

"He could have been hit from behind?"

Jack tilted his head. "Makes sense, right? I'm sure that's what they're thinking down there. Blow to the back of the head — always suspicious."

Sarah turned to the shore.

The SOCO was still walking around the boat, bent over. Alan meanwhile had raced back to the police car.

Yes, they had found something.

Jack summed it up. "The mayor goes to the island for some reason we don't have a clue about. And while he's there, someone bashes him on the back of the skull. Slips the body into the water knowing it will look like he fell on those rocks."

"Wait. Someone went in the boat with him?"

Jack shook his head. "No, I mean, how could they? The boat Laurent used is still there on the island. Which means they used the other boat — the one down there."

As Sarah watched, the SOCO walked back to join Alan and the two started conferring.

They'd definitely found something interesting.

"You need to see any more, Jack?" said Sarah. "Only I ought to be getting back."

"No, I'm done. Plenty to think about here."

AS THEY PULLED up in the village square, Sarah's phone rang.

"Bet that's Daniel," she said.

Jack nodded and turned the engine off.

Sarah slid her phone out of her jeans, but it wasn't her son calling. "Tony, hi, we've talked to Lady Repton and—"

"Sarah."

She stopped. Tony's voice was tense, tight. "They've just

arrested Simon Repton for the murder of Laurent Bourdin."

She put the phone on speaker, Jack's gaze locked on her, things happening so fast now. "They found a bloody hand print on one of the boats, Simon's apparently. Didn't even deny it was his. But he claims to be totally innocent!"

"God," she said.

"Lady Repton, well, she is beside herself, as I'm sure you can imagine. She called me; I said I would get in touch with you."

"Tony, do you think—"

"Sarah, I don't know *what* to think. But I'm afraid this is a murder case now. You think you and Jack might carry on?"

She looked at Jack, the sun on his face, the lines there deep as he watched and listened so carefully.

He nodded to her. "Sure, Tony. Not sure what we can do though, with an arrest, and the police involved."

"Thank you, Sarah. It's Lady Repton I'm thinking about. This could destroy her."

Jack leaned close to the phone.

Did he suspect Simon as well?

"Tony," Jack said, "we'll see what we can do."

A noisy group of children came out of the newsagents, laughing and joking as they passed the car.

"Thank you too, Jack. And if there's anything I can do, let me know."

"Will do, Tony," Sarah said. "Bye for now."

She ended the call.

Jack looked around at the placid village square. He nodded, as if the call had confirmed all the thoughts he had been having. Then he turned back to Sarah.

"So, Sarah — appears we have a case after all."

8.

A PARTY OF SUSPECTS

SARAH SAT IN the lounge of the King's Head Hotel and thumbed through a copy of *Country Life*. Apart from an old couple having tea in the far corner, the place was empty.

Perfect, she thought.

At the height of summer, this hotel — right in the centre of Cherringham — was usually full. But now, on a drab Tuesday morning, she could hardly think of anywhere better to interview a possible witness to a murder.

Better certainly than the bare room at Cherringham police station where she'd just spent an hour with Alan Rivers going through her own statement. She doubted whether anything she'd said would be used in an eventual trial: she'd given her presentation, had dinner and was long gone before Laurent Bourdin met his fate.

But now it was time for her to ask the questions…

Right on cue, Marie Duval appeared at the doorway of the lounge. Sarah hardly recognised her: dark sunglasses, hair in a tight bun, a Hermes scarf round her neck and an elegant black suit. It was quite a transformation.

Mourning chic… thought Sarah and then instantly regretted being so uncharitable.

She stood up and Marie nodded and came over to join her at the little table by the French windows.

"I'm so sorry," said Sarah as Marie kissed her on each cheek. "How are you, Marie?"

"To be honest, I don't really know," said Marie, sitting on the sofa opposite. "It's all been like a bad dream. Or worse — a *cauchemar!*"

"A nightmare. Yes, I can understand that. Is there anything I can do for you?"

"You're so kind," said Marie, placing her hands on her lap, folding the ends of her scarf together. "But the hotel here has been wonderful. They're looking after me."

"You didn't want to stay at the Hall? I'm sure Lady Repton—"

"No, I really had to get out of that place."

Sarah waited for Marie to take her sunglasses off, but she clearly wasn't going to.

"I've ordered tea — I hope that's all right?"

"Of course. Tea. The English answer to everything, yes?"

Sarah smiled briefly — and then, as the waitress appeared with the tray, she sat back while the tea was poured.

She watched Marie, who sat impassive.

It was hard to believe this was the same person who'd conga'ed through Repton Hall just three nights ago, hair flowing, head back, laughing and flirting with the Cherringham councillors.

Simon had hinted that Marie and Laurent had more than a working relationship.

So this must be hitting her hard, thought Sarah.

"I really do appreciate you agreeing to talk to me, Marie," she said. "At such a difficult time."

"It's what Laurent would have wanted," said Marie.

"I assume the police have already interviewed you?"

Marie nodded, but didn't look up at Sarah. Instead she stared at the tea in the pretty little cup in front of her. Sarah watched as she folded the corners of her silk scarf over and over again, her whole body still but her hands moving constantly.

"Have you heard from Monsieur Bourdin's wife and family?" said Sarah.

"His wife is in the Far East, a business trip," said Marie. "I gather she will be here at the end of the week. He has no children."

"When will you go back to France?"

"The police have asked me not to leave," said Marie with a sigh. "*Pourquoi?* But I planned to stay anyway. Until the signing."

Sarah wondered how to move the subject on, but Marie did the job for her.

"Laurent's wife and I... how can I say? She tolerated me. In the way French wives do."

"I had heard, that you and Laurent were... close..."

"*Bien sur!* We were lovers — you can say the word, Sarah. In France it is not such a big issue."

"So his death must have been a shock."

"Laurent? He was my guiding star. He was everything to me. But when *she* arrives, I shall step aside. That is what lovers do."

Sarah watched as Marie seemed to crumple a little. She decided she was just going to have to be bold, keep the conversation going.

"I hope you don't mind me asking you this — but have you any idea why Laurent went down to the lake that night?"

"He smoked cigars, the occasional cigarette. So he often went outside in the evening. Maybe he went for a walk, a smoke."

"The police think he took a boat — and went out to the island."

"Hmm? No, that's not possible. Laurent grew up by the sea. He understood water — and its dangers. He wouldn't go rowing across a lake in the middle of the night." She took a breath. "Not after so much wine. Why would he do that?"

"You know that Simon Repton has been arrested," said Sarah.

"They told me."

"You don't sound surprised."

"Nothing surprises me about that night."

"When I left, the mood seemed to be high-spirited. Did things change?"

Sarah watched Marie carefully. The other woman seemed to be choosing her words.

"Yes. A small group of us — we stayed up late, having fun."

"In the hot tub, I hear."

"It sounds worse than it was. Just silly games. A little harmless flirting, I suppose. Everybody was doing it. So much wine."

"Not just wine — at least that's what I hear."

"It's possible. Not me. But maybe… the men. A little."

"Who was there?"

"Laurent. Mr. Howden. Simon. Mr. Jones. June. But Laurent got annoyed for some reason. Simon made a joke of it, but that made Laurent even more angry and he went off on his own."

"You don't know why?"

"Laurent, well he often got in a mood about things. He could be quite jealous. I've learned to ignore it."

"So what happened then?"

"Simon went to look for him. And I went to bed."

"Did Laurent join you, later?"

"No."

Marie looked away.

Was that guilt over not looking for Laurent? Or was just the memory too painful? The next morning, the body…

Had to be grisly.

"But you weren't worried?"

"I was tired. I put my earplugs in and went straight to sleep. When I woke in the morning there was no sign of him or his clothes."

"So what did you think had happened to him?"

"I assumed I'd find him downstairs on a sofa. Asleep. Instead, it seems Simon was the last person to see him…" She shook her head. "I don't understand it at all."

And then Marie suddenly started to cry. Sarah quickly got up and sat next to her on the sofa, putting a hand on her shoulder to comfort her. Marie opened her handbag, took out a silk handkerchief and wiped her eyes under her sunglasses and dabbed her nose.

"I'm sorry," said Marie.

"You mustn't be."

Sarah watched as Marie began folding and re-folding the ends of her silk scarf again, her hands now the only indication that emotions had been stirred underneath that cool exterior.

Sarah waited. Letting the tears ebb. She wondered if she should end this.

What would Jack do?

He'd ask her more questions — even at this vulnerable moment.

"Was Laurent completely committed to the twinning?" said Sarah.

Maria seemed surprised.

"Of course! He and I worked nearly two years for this deal. Why would you ask such a question?"

"Because apparently on Saturday night Laurent threatened to pull out."

"That's ridiculous," said Marie. "Absurd! Whoever told you that is lying. The twinning was good for everyone. For St. Martin, for Cherringham…"

"For business…"

"Yes of course, for business," said Marie and Sarah now saw a flicker of the tough politician she'd been told existed under the charming surface. "Win-win as you English say. We are not charities Sarah — and twinning is not just an exercise in European solidarity. There are tangible benefits which can be measured and which accrue from such arrangements."

"Of course — I didn't mean to suggest there was anything underhand going on—"

"Good," said Marie, now looking directly at Sarah. "Laurent and I put everything into building this relationship, as did your own council. I would hate to think that our selfless commitment, and all our time and effort to the project, could be damaged by his death."

Sarah was taken by surprise by this sudden drift into formal statements: it was as if Marie was rehearsing her lines for a press release.

As if she'd been rehearsing before this very meeting… "Marie, you must forgive me. Lady Repton… she is a friend. She asked for my help, and my friend, Jack."

Marie's eyes narrowed at that.

Alarm? Interesting.

"All we want to do is find out what happened to Laurent. I certainly don't have any view on the rights or wrongs of the twinning."

Sarah watched as Marie opened her handbag, took out her handkerchief again, dabbed her nose, then put the handkerchief away again.

"Lady Repton has asked you to help?"

"Yes," said Sarah. "Especially now with her grandson arrested."

"You're working for her?"

"Advising her. Helping her."

"*D'accord.* So — you are trying to get Simon, how do you say — *off the hook*, yes?"

"Trying to find the truth, Marie."

"But do you think he had something to do with Laurent's death?"

"Right now," said Sarah, "I don't know."

"Simon wanted the twinning even more than we did! But if Laurent really had changed his mind..."

Sarah wondered whether Marie was beginning to think of Simon as the killer.

The classic question.

If someone murdered Laurent, *why?*

"What happens now, Marie? Do you think the twinning deal is off?"

"Non! Why? The ceremony was planned for Friday. In Laurent's absence I am completely authorised to sign. Unless I hear otherwise — the twinning goes ahead."

With that, Marie gathered her handbag and stood up.

"But I am tired now. All these questions."

She reached across to shake Sarah's hand.

And as she did, her scarf fell open and Sarah could see, clearly, a rough bruise on her neck. Marie quickly pulled the scarf tight again and Sarah looked away.

She didn't have that mark on her neck on Saturday night, thought Sarah.

"I am sorry I've had to ask you difficult questions, Marie," said Sarah, smiling as sympathetically as she could.

"You must do what you must do. For your friend. But I hope — at least for the rest of this week — you will be able to leave me in peace, non?"

"Of course," said Sarah. "You've been very helpful."

Sarah watched Marie leave the lounge and thought hard about the mark she'd seen on her neck.

She's been helpful all right. But has she been completely honest?
Sarah couldn't wait to talk this over with Jack.

9.

TALKING TURKEY

JACK DROVE DOWN the long straight road toward the turkey farm. With the top down — and the wind clearly blowing in this direction — he could already smell the place, and it sure wasn't pleasant.

Thank God this is the other side of Cherringham from the Grey Goose, he thought, the rich, fetid smell already making him feel queasy.

He pulled up at the main entrance. On either side of the road, a long line of tall fencing disappeared into the distance, like the wire round a prison camp.

As Jack waited for one of the uniformed guards to come over and let him in, he could hear a distant low, gurgling hum coming from the large sheds, scattered across the fields on the other side of this gate.

It was, he guessed, the noise of a hundred thousand turkeys having their dinner. For some, their last meal.

It's good not to be a turkey.

Searching online, Jack had learned that just twenty years ago this road had been a runway — one of the longest in Europe — and it would have been USAAF bombers rather than turkeys making the noise.

Jack's great uncle had been a flyer in WW2. Gunner in B52s. Who knew — maybe the guy had even flown into this base.

Wouldn't that be something? What a time that must have been, for the young pilots, for the whole world.

Jack looked up to the grey clouds, low over the far hill and thought of all those Americans who'd stood where he stood and watched planes coming in to land.

Through the war, and on into the Cold War.

Thirty years ago his own American accent wouldn't have turned a head.

Long connection we have with this place, he thought.

In some ways, maybe I'm not such an outsider.

Jack knew from his morning's research that as the Cold War dwindled, the bombers had gone home, or been redeployed. Finally, even the RAF had decided there was no need for it — especially as there was another base just a few miles away.

According to Wikipedia, the place had closed, and the land had been sold — to an ambitious young farmer by the name of Harry Howden.

It seemed that Harry had seen the chance to expand his free-range turkey business. And Harry's timing turned out to be impeccable. Jack was no fan of massive industrial farms like this — but he had to admire Harry's self-belief.

The guy had been right — and Harry Howden was now one of the richest food producers in the country. Thanks to those countless turkeys who even now were readying themselves to lay down their lives for the Howden brand.

"Jack Brennan. I'm here to see Mr. Howden," said Jack, as the gate security guard leaned down to the little Sprite.

Jack watched as the guard tapped instructions into a pad.

"Right. Mr. Howden says he'll see you up at the house, sir," said the guard impassively.

"And where might that be?"

Jack followed the guard's outstretched hand, as he pointed towards a big modern building set up on a hill overlooking the airfield.

"Just drive round the airfield sir, then follow the lane up into the woods. You can't miss it."

HARRY HOWDEN WAS waiting for Jack when he pulled up on the tarmac frontage of the immaculate Howden residence.

As Jack got out of the car, Howden came over to shake his hand and introduce himself.

"Nice place," said Jack, looking at the big house when the introductions were over. "Very different for the area."

"You *bet* it's different. Built to my own specification," said Harry. "And the wife's of course."

"Of course."

"To be honest, my only real stipulation was that I wanted to be able to see the farm from all the main rooms. You need to watch your investment, you know."

All those turkeys under Harry's watchful gaze.

Jack turned and looked down into the valley. Harry had got his wish: from up here the triangle of runways was clearly visible, as were the dozen or so enormous turkey barns that spread across them.

"And how did your wife feel about that?"

"She's never forgiven me," said Harry with a smile. "Likes the money, but not so keen on seeing all those barns from every window!"

Jack could see the steel underneath that smile.

"Why not put the barns all together?" asked Jack, changing the subject. "Sell the rest of the land — you surely don't need it all."

"Contagion," said Harry. "Got to keep a minimum distance between the barns — Bird Flu, health, safety. Lots of turkey factories don't give a damn about that. Thousands of young birds die in the first week."

He looked right at Jack. "I wanted something better. Besides — I've got plans for the gaps in between."

"More livestock?"

"God no. I'm nearly up to a hundred-and-fifty-thousand birds as it is. No, I'm putting in for wind turbines."

"Blow the smell away, huh?"

Jack watched Harry carefully; interested to see how he took this comment.

"Ha! Very good!" said Harry, laughing loudly. "Truth is —
after all these years you don't notice the smell at all. Least I don't.
Mrs. Howden though…"

Harry laughed.

"So your plan for the turbines, that for the good of the local
environment?"

"For the good of my profits, I hope. We're also recycling all the
droppings. Mixed with wood chips makes a great fuel. Going to
build a methane plant."

Jack realised he was learning more about raising turkeys than
he ever thought he would, or wanted to.

"Makes sense. Customers want green these days — and they
want their meat looked after nicely." Jack turned to look over the
expansive field and sheds. "Nice operation you have here."

"Thanks. And I don't blame those customers," said Harry. "It's
a short life being a turkey on one of my farms. I don't begrudge
them a bit of comfort. Going free-range too — partly. You can
taste the difference."

Jack nodded, hoping that he could end this part of the
conversation. He wanted to get down to the real business of his
visit.

"Anyway," said Harry. "Enough talking turkey." Another
laugh. "Let's grab a coffee."

And with that he turned on his heels and climbed the shiny
brick steps to his double-fronted house as Jack followed.

"TELL YOU HARRY, this sofa of yours is as big as my sitting
room," said Jack.

Harry laughed. "You live down on the river, don't you?"

"Got an old Dutch barge."

"Must be great fun. Like it here in ye olde England?" said
Harry, clearing a pile of French books out of the way and putting
a mug of coffee down in front of Jack.

Jack watched as the big man sank back in a massive white
leather armchair opposite.

"Most of the time," said Jack, suddenly realising that instead of doing the interviewing, he was being interviewed himself...

This guy's either clever — or he's genuine, thought Jack. Time to take control.

He took out a small notepad and pen. Over the years he'd found it to be a very useful accessory.

Kinda focuses the mind.

It had an immediate effect.

"Notebook? I wonder if I should have my lawyer here," said Harry. "Just kidding, Jack — Tony said I could trust you. So I will."

"That's good of him," said Jack. "Just want to ask a few questions. Trying to help Lady Repton."

"Fire away," said Harry. "We'll have to be quick, mind — my wife will be home soon and I'm under orders to take her out to dinner tonight."

"Sure," said Jack. "No problem. So why don't we start with the obvious question..."

"Do I think Simon Repton killed Laurent Bourdin?"

"That's the one."

"No, I don't."

"You sound pretty sure."

"Oh, I am. Simon Repton doesn't have the balls."

"Who does?"

"Lee Jones. That French bird, the deputy mayor. Or even June Rigby. Cold one, she is."

"You?"

Harry laughed. "Of course — but you knew that already."

It was Jack's turn to laugh.

"So — in your opinion — where does that leave us?" said Jack.

"Motive, of course," said Harry. "But you know that. NYPD and all. Now see, that's where it gets tricky, though."

"Go on."

"Well, as far as I'm aware, every single one of us 'suspects' wants the twinning to go ahead. *Needs* the twinning, you might say. For various business reasons — we're all into this up to our necks.

So killing Laurent wouldn't benefit any of us, would it? Could jeopardise the whole thing."

"No," said Jack. "But what if I told you Laurent was going to pull out of the twinning?"

Jack watched as this piece of news sunk in — Harry clearly didn't know this, or if he did he was seriously a good poker player.

"That doesn't make sense. His village needs it as well. When did he change his mind?"

"Saturday night, apparently."

"Shit," said Harry. "If that's the case, it changes everything. Who knew?"

"Simon certainly. Marie claims she didn't. The others — I don't yet know."

"So what the hell else do you know? Damn. Is the twinning off?"

"Marie is ready to sign on Friday apparently. You'll have to talk to the council to see if their plans have changed."

Jack watched him carefully.

"You got a lot riding on this Harry?"

"Absolutely. About five million. Nothing illegal, mind. But Laurent assured me the twinning would help my inward investment in the St. Martin food processing industry."

"Smooth the wheels, huh?"

"Exactly. So I need this little episode sorted and fast. Little over-extended on my lines of credit. Shit. You're sure Marie's still on board?"

"Harry, this isn't my business. It's just something I heard."

"Yeah, yeah. God."

Harry got up, and Jack watched him as he went to the window and looked down upon his empire, the lines of turkey barns stretching into the misty distance.

"Maybe whoever killed Laurent had nothing to do with us?" said Harry, not turning round. "You know, some guy just passing through. Druggie or whatever…"

"Anything's possible. But it's pretty unlikely, Harry. Three in the morning on a deserted country estate? No, my guess is it's someone you know. If it isn't you, of course."

"You damn well know it wasn't me. Maybe it *was* Simon."

Bit of a backtrack there…

"Why don't you tell me what happened that night?"

When Harry turned to face him, Jack could see that the man's tough exterior had been pierced by the news of Laurent's about-face.

This five million deal is higher stakes than he's making out, thought Jack. *The guy's rattled…*

And really rattled people can do anything.

HARRY WALKED JACK through the evening — the champagne reception, the presentation, the dinner… Everything normal, above board, a lot of drink consumed but then as Harry put it:

"I've been involved with this thing for the last two years and I've never seen people drink as much as they did on Saturday. And the other stuff, well…"

"Other stuff?"

Harry paused and Jack could sense he was uncertain how much to give away.

"You've talked to the others about this, haven't you?"

"The coke. That what you mean, Harry?"

"It was like an end-of-term party, you know? Madness."

"I can imagine."

"Here's the thing, Jack," he said, leaning across conspiratorially. "We've had a few trips to St. Martin over the last year or two. And let's just say people's moral compasses have got a bit disorientated on occasion."

"Yours too?"

"Good God, no, I'm happily married, me," said Harry quickly. "But Lee for instance — I know for a fact he had the hots for that deputy mayor, Marie. And it sure looked like it was reciprocated."

Jack nodded, man to man.

"I mean, I don't blame him mind, she's quite a looker," he continued. "But I did have to warn him off — for the sake of the whole deal, you know."

"What was the big deal? She's a single woman, no?" said Jack innocently.

"You've got to be joking. She and Laurent were an item," said Harry. "Don't want to lay the goose that's laying the golden egg!"

There's a joke in those words, Jack thought.

But Harry was certainly in no joking mood. "I see. What about Simon? What did he get up to on those trips?"

"Good question. I think he had a hankering for the same fruit. But our Lee wasn't going to let that happen. And like I said — Simon's not a dog I'd back in a fight. He backed off sharpish and looked elsewhere, so I hear."

"Anyone in particular?"

"There were five of us in that hot tub Jack — you do the math as you Americans say."

"I see," said Jack, making a note in his notepad. "Do you think Laurent realised, by the way?"

"What? About Lee? Well, that's the thing, you see. We'd only been in the hot tub for—"

"Not that damned hot tub again, Harry," came a powerful female voice from behind them. "Puh-lease."

Jack turned. A tall, stocky woman in her forties in a long dark expensive-looking coat stood in the doorway.

"Vanessa, my *dear*," said Harry getting up. "I didn't hear your car…"

"Too busy boring our guest with salacious stories, I suspect," said Vanessa coming over to Jack and offering her hand.

"Vanessa Howden," she said.

"Jack Brennan."

"Ah, the famous American detective."

"Ex-detective," said Jack carefully. "And not famous by any stretch of the imagination."

"Jack's trying to find out a little about Saturday night, my dear," said Harry. Jack sensed that Harry had an alpha rival in his wife.

Interesting…

"He's working for Lady Repton," added Harry.

And Jack made a note of that. He hadn't told Harry about the Repton connection when he'd made the appointment to see him. News travelled fast in Cherringham — he knew that. But somebody had phoned Harry, warned him what Jack was up to.

"Oh really?" said Vanessa. "Well I'm not sure there's anything we can tell you that we haven't already told the police, Mr. Brennan."

"Harry was just talking about the hot tub."

She rolled her eyes. "I know."

"But you weren't there, Mrs. Howden?"

"I went to bed after the dinner. Hot tubs are not for me."

Jack turned to the now-cowed husband. "But Harry, you carried on partying — so perhaps –?"

Vanessa didn't take her eyes off Jack as she spoke: "As I'm sure Harry told you, he only stayed for a few minutes with the others and then he too came to bed."

Jack looked from Vanessa to her husband. Harry seemed confused, standing next to Vanessa, her face set, unreadable.

Something going on here, he thought.

"That right, Harry?" said Jack.

"Yes, th-that's right."

"Really? I thought you hung out for a little longer in the tub with the party crowd?"

"Good lord, no. Not at my age."

Too quick with that.

Jack made another note.

"I mean, obviously I could hear them all in there. Very noisy! Music and all sorts!"

"But you didn't stay…"

"Dipped my toes. Thought better of it. Back to the room, cup of tea, lights out. Isn't that right, Vanessa?"

"Absolutely," said Vanessa, just as quickly. "So I'm not sure how we can help you, Mr. Brennan. Such a tragic event of course. And even more desperate to hear that Simon Repton himself may have been somehow involved. You must give my condolences to

Lady Repton when you see her."

"I will," said Jack, closing his notepad. Vanessa Howden's body language made it completely clear: it was time for him to go.

She smiled at him and nodded towards the door.

"Now you'll have to forgive me," she said. "But Harry and I have a social engagement and we mustn't be late. So I'm terribly sorry..."

Jack knew what it meant when English hosts said that.

It meant get your sorry ass out of here.

But Jack wasn't quite ready to leave. At the front door, he took out his notepad and pen and turned sharply to Vanessa, surprising her.

"Sorry — just for the record Mrs. Howden — when precisely was the last time you saw Laurent Bourdin?"

The move — and the question — had exactly the result he wanted. For the first time, Vanessa looked confused. She swallowed — turned to Harry who stood beside her, clearly seeking help.

"At the dinner," she said.

Nice. Composure blown.

"Um, no Vanessa," said Harry quickly. "After the dinner but before we all — they all — went off to get swimming costumes."

"So then — before Sarah left?" asked Jack quickly.

"What?" said Vanessa. "No, after."

This was great. Their story was in tatters.

"Yes, after," said Harry.

Jack smiled at them both, and made another note in his notepad.

"Good," said Jack, putting away his pad and pen with a smile. "That was very helpful."

He turned and headed down the steps at the front of the house to his car, aware that Harry and Vanessa must still be at the open door looking down at him.

Boy, I wish I could see their faces, he thought.

Because the turkey farmer and his wife were lying through their teeth.

That was good.

Now all I gotta do is work out why.

And with that, he climbed into the Sprite and sped away back to Cherringham.

10.

SMOOTH OPERATOR

SARAH PULLED OFF the main road and parked next to the long line of smart black SUVs which fronted Jones & Co — 4WD Specialists.

As she got out and hurried to the sales office, she looked back across the forecourt: her mud-splattered old Rav-4, with its dents and stickers, its little orange foam ball on the aerial and its missing hubcap, certainly lowered the tone of the whole place.

She couldn't help but smile. That car was nearly as old as the kids and she wasn't ever going to get rid of it.

That was something her budget wouldn't allow.

As she entered the reception area she could tell instantly that this was not your average second-hand car dealership.

She looked around: smart sofas, deep carpets, glass shelves with trophies and awards — and not a pin-up calendar in sight.

But the whole place was strangely empty. The reception area was ringed by a series of small glass-walled offices — all empty too. She checked her watch — it was nine a.m.

And Lee Jones had assured her he was going to be here. Sarah needed to be back at the office at nine-thirty — back to her real, paying job — and she didn't have time to waste.

So where was everybody?

Then she heard raised voices. An argument echoing from the back of the garage. Off to a corner she saw a door marked "Service and Parts". She went over and opened the door — and walked right in.

What would Jack call this?

Chutzpah…

It led to a small corridor and another door.

She found herself in the middle of what looked like a labour meeting, and it didn't seem to be going well.

A dozen workers — mechanics in overalls, salesmen in suits — stood in a rough circle, arms folded, tempers up. And in front of them — Lee Jones, shirt sleeves, hands full of paperwork, gesturing as if to pacify this angry crowd.

"I've made guarantees, now, haven't I? I've given my word and I don't want any more of this, this *crap*, now—"

Sarah watched as he noticed her at the door and spun round.

"What the — Sarah? How did you…?"

"I'm sorry, Lee — there was nobody on reception — I just thought I'd better find you," said Sarah, aware that the whole room had turned to her.

Bad timing, she thought.

Lee jumped on a reason to escape the meeting.

"No problem, no problem."

He turned to his workforce. "I'm sorry fellas; I have to take this meeting. We'll carry on at lunch — okay? Until then, please, just concentrate on hitting these damn schedules — all right?"

There was a lot of muttering and shaking of heads as the group slouched off.

Lee turned to her, gave a sigh and ushered her back towards his office. No question that he was grateful for her unexpected arrival.

"Nick of time, Sarah. They were ready to eat me alive!"

"I ENVY YOU Sarah. Nice little business you've got, no staff problems, come and go when you like…"

Sarah watched as Lee leaned back in his leather executive office chair and put his hands behind his head, comfortable now he was back in his own office.

She could have told him that running a family as a single mum and steering her design company single-handed through a recession was no piece of cake, but she wanted Lee to feel in charge.

Comfortable. Safe…

That way he might tell her something useful.

So she smiled and shrugged. "Can't have been easy for you these last couple of years," she said.

"Too bloody right," he said straight away. "But you try telling that lot back there. And now all they want to talk about is wage increases? It's like the bleedin' seventies all over again. If it wasn't for me they wouldn't have a bloody wage to increase. Know what I mean?"

"So is business bad?"

"It's been better. Some weeks, it feels like we're coming out of it. Others, you can hear the paint drying in here! But if they think they're going to hold me hostage wanting more money — well, the hell they will."

"Must be a lot of money, I mean, tied up in all those cars sitting out there?"

"Tell me about it. I've got to shift three a month just to cover the overheads. Thirty K a pop, that's a lot of pennies sitting in the rain waiting for a buyer."

"Lot of euros."

That made Lee pause.

"Well — there you have it, Sarah, there you have it, hmm? You've got to be in it to win it, as they say — and that's why *moi, j'aime les francaises!*"

"That's very good, Lee, you've obviously got a gift for languages."

"Not the only gift I got," he said, leaning forwards and giving her what she guessed was his best seductive smile. "Shame you didn't stay on Saturday you know, you might have had fun…"

Jack had told Sarah on the phone about his little chat with Harry Howden, so she knew that Lee fancied himself as a bit of a ladies' man.

She smiled back politely. "Sadly, I've got two teenagers to bring up, Lee — fun's not so high on my priorities these days."

And with that, we'll change the subject, thought Sarah.

"You've had your police interview I suppose?"

She watched him frown.

"Waste of bloody time that was."

"You couldn't help them then?"

"What do you think? Think I'm going to just say — it was Lord Repton in the library with the spanner?"

He got up and poured himself some water from a cooler in the corner of the office, then came over and sat opposite Sarah on a small sofa.

"So then — what do you think did happen that night?" she said.

"Know what? I think Laurent just… fell in the lake. He was well pissed. I mean, I can put it away with the best of them, but jeez… Laurent was chucking down brandies even while he was sitting in the hot tub."

"And you don't think Simon had anything to do with it?"

"Ah, now, don't get me wrong. I'm not saying that. The two of them did have quite a barney."

"You know what it was about?"

"I didn't then. Most of it happened later on in the bar, I gather. But from what I've heard since, Laurent suddenly wanted out of the whole deal."

"And you don't know why?"

"Not a clue, I'm afraid. One minute all brothers in arms, next minute shouting his head off and storming out."

"What was he saying before he went off?"

"You do like asking questions, don't you," He shook his head. "No idea really. To be honest — *deux bieres, s'il vous plait* — that's my limit. Full-on slanging match? I didn't understand a word."

"But you must have seen who was he shouting at?"

"Who *wasn't* he yelling at? Me, Marie, June, Harry — as I said, totally pissed."

"Er — Harry was there?"

"Sure."

"And Simon?"

"Yeah, him too. The 'Famous Five' we called ourselves. All for one and one for all… least when it came to the twinning deal."

"So what happened when Laurent stormed off?"

"We had a bit of a laugh to be honest, opened another bottle of bubbly, which none of us needed."

"He didn't come back?"

"Not as far as I know." Lee looked away. "Last I saw of him."

"Did you stay long in the hot tub?"

"Had another drink — then I went to bed."

"And the hot tubbers left?"

"Umm… June. Harry. Marie."

"Simon?"

Lee looked up. "No. Simon went off to find Laurent. You know; gracious host and all that."

"But he didn't come back?"

"Well, how would I know? You did hear me, yes? Like I said, I'd gone to bed."

Sarah sat calmly trying to line up everybody's accounts of that night in her head.

None of it fitting together.

And maybe — no one telling the truth.

"Do you know why Simon did go after Laurent?"

"French mayor angry. *Le deal* in jeopardy… Simon had most to lose I guess."

"In what way?"

"Simon's got plans, hasn't he? A big resort hotel just outside St. Martin, that's what I heard."

Interesting. And Sarah could guess where that money came from.

"You think he invested some of Lady Repton's money on the basis of the twinning going ahead?" said Sarah.

Lee sat back, and Sarah watched as he seemed to be weighing up what to say to her. Then he leaned forward again.

"Hang on." Lee nodded as if had just shrewdly figured out a problem. Then a finger wag at Sarah. "You're working for Simon, aren't you?"

"No. Not at all. For Lady Repton — as a favour."

"Hmm."

For the first time, Sarah felt she might be getting close to what had really happened.

He knows something, something important…

"Lee, if you've got information, you have to tell me. It's bound to come out in the end."

A long pause. Lee weighing things. Seductiveness gone, caginess in.

A deep breath, then he leaned close.

"All right," he said. "But you didn't hear this from me, okay?"

"Sure."

"You know the twinning's important — for all of us — for business reasons, yes?"

"Sure. Makes sense. You, Cecil, Simon, Harry, you all stand to benefit."

"Exactly — the whole village, really — *if* the twinning goes ahead. But do you know why — and how — we all benefit?"

"Business, I suppose. Opportunities."

Lee laughed.

"I like that. Opportunities. That's about the measure of it. But here's the thing: opportunities don't come free in the real world, Sarah. Sometimes you have to pay for them."

"I don't understand," she said, though in truth she was beginning to. This whole twinning thing was a financial web.

And Laurent had been about to cut all the strands.

"Laurent Bourdin had his hands in the till. Every construction, every land sale, every deal that went on in that pretty little town of his — he took a cut."

"Bribes?"

Lee nodded.

"What sort of money are we talking about?"

"Oh tons. Twenty grand. Thirty. Fifty…"

"From *everyone*?"

Lee shrugged.

"And you all paid up?"

"Not me."

Was that the truth?

"But the others did?"

"So I hear."

Sarah paused while this information sank in.

"Did you tell the police this?" she said.

"Come on! You've got to be kidding."

"It does give Simon a real motive."

Lee shrugged.

"I like Simon. Yes, he's a bit of an upper-class twit, sure. But underneath all that he's okay. For a twit."

Sarah nodded. "So why did you just tell me all this?"

"Because if you're going to help him, and his grandmother, you need to know everything that was 'in play'. He sure as hell isn't going to tell you himself."

Sarah nodded slowly. Lee got up — he wasn't going to tell her any more.

"Anyway," said Lee, looking at his watch. "I've got a nine-thirty appointment, so if you don't mind; I've got cars to sell."

"Yes. I need to get back to work, too," said Sarah, getting up.

They shook hands and Lee escorted her out to the garage forecourt, then, with a wave, went back inside.

A cold breeze was blowing outside, and Sarah pulled up the collar of her coat. She went over to her car, climbed in and put the heater on.

But before she pulled away, she sat still, watching the traffic whizz by on the main road, thinking through what she'd just discovered.

Up to now she'd found it impossible to see why Simon Repton would possibly want to murder Laurent.

But this information changed everything.

What Lee just told her was completely damning of Simon.

Had she and Jack got it all wrong?

Was Simon really the killer?

It suddenly seemed that way …

11.

DINNER AND QUESTIONS

SARAH HEARD THE knock on the door. She had only arrived home a few minutes before, and Jack was here already.

He had proposed meeting at The Angel, but she needed to make sure Daniel and Chloe were sorted with their schoolwork.

Being a mum came first, and Jack knew that.

She opened the door.

Jack held up a bottle. "Brought some wine, if that's okay. Something called a 'baby Barolo'." He looked at the label. "Italian."

She smiled as he walked in. "Sounds good to me. Nothing special for dinner tonight, you know. Just last night's lasagne doing a repeat performance."

"And *that* sounds perfect to me."

He put the bottle on the table, and just stood there for a second. Such a big guy, in that small kitchen. But she always had the feeling that Jack enjoyed these visits to her little home, with her two kids.

Something he missed.

And the kids — they always enjoyed when the American detective came over — NYPD!

"Corkscrew?" he asked.

"Top drawer," she said, opening the oven door to check if the lasagne had started bubbling.

Then Chloe ran in, waving a paper in her hand. "Mum! This is the trip I told you about! Can you look at it?"

"Evening, Chloe," Jack said.

Her daughter spun around and smiled. "Oh — hi Mr. Brennan!" Then quickly back to Sarah.

Sarah knew what the paper was all about.

"It's got all the info on the trip there. Can we think about me going?" Sarah took the paper, then looked at Jack.

"The school orchestra is sponsoring a trip to your hometown, Jack. They're going to play some concerts, see the sights."

"Wow. Sounds exciting."

Sarah nodded, checking the cost in bold at the bottom of the page.

"And pricey."

Chloe was wide-eyed with the possibility. But — no doubt — it was a lot of money.

"I'll save all my babysitting money. I swear. And I'll even look for more babysitting."

Sarah nodded. "I... *we*... will think and talk about it."

A little light went out of Chloe's eyes.

"It sounds like a great trip, Chloe." Sarah added. Then: "I'd love you to go."

Chloe nodded. Sarah knew she would be as good as her word about saving all that money.

And Sarah supposed she could cut a few corners as well.

"Could you tell Daniel that dinner is ready?"

Then Chloe did what every kid would do.

Top of her lungs.

"Daniel! Dinner!"

Daniel and Chloe had cleared the table, then vanished back to their rooms.

The wine had been rich, delicious.

Really special, Sarah thought.

"Hope Chloe can do that trip," Jack said. "I could give her a lot of tips on what to see and do."

"I hope so, too."

Jack hesitated. Then: "If there's anything, er, I can do to help that little project along, let me know. Always been a big supporter of educational field trips."

She smiled at that. So... *Jack.*

Then, sitting at the cleared table, he dug out his notebook, and flipped it open.

"Shall we see what we got here?"

"We need a notebook, Jack?"

"Case like this? Everyone with a motive, it seems. My memory isn't what it used to be so thought I'd better do this 'old school'."

Then he began going through the roster of those at the twinning reception, the dinner, the hot tub nonsense afterwards.

"Do a timeline of the evening — and everybody has a different story."

"They've all got something to hide," said Sarah.

"One thing's for sure. Nobody wanted that deal to go down. And everyone had a financial interest."

"Some pretty dire, I guess," Sarah said. "I think Lee's got cash problems up at the garage."

"Harry Howden's in up to his neck too, I'd wager."

"So, Lee, Harry... And Marie's got some secrets — I'm sure of it. You know there's an emergency parish council meeting tonight?"

"Really? Guess the village elders can't let a mere floating corpse get in the way of a good deal. Can you find out what happened?"

"I should be able to — whatever it is, they'll want it in the newsletter. June Rigby is in charge of council minutes. I'm sure she'll call."

Sarah reached for the bottle, and started to pour another glass for Jack.

"No. You go on, though. I've been thinking about this - everyone with a motive... We're still missing something. Just a hunch."

"I've come to pay attention to those."

"Like that island. Laurent going out there. I mean, why?"

Sarah's mobile phone trilled.

"Hang on," she said. "I'll let it go to message if it's not—"

She slid the phone out.

"It's Tony."

"Tad late to be calling. Must be something up."

"Tony, Jack's here, mind if I put you on speaker?"

"Sure. Absolutely."

"Hi Tony," Jack said. "We were just talking about what we've learned. Which — I'm afraid — isn't much."

"Jack, Sarah... Lady Repton just called. In *tears*! Absolutely sobbing."

"Why?" Sarah said. "What's happened?"

"Simon has been formally charged with the murder of Laurent Bourdin. They found evidence tying him to the crime — and it is now most definitely a crime."

Sarah looked at Jack. Just as he was talking about pieces being missing, and now this.

"Tony," Jack said. "Did Lady Repton say what they found?"

"Yes. A tyre iron. Bloody, with Simon's prints all over it. The murder weapon, apparently."

"That's not good," Sarah said.

But her eyes were on Jack. He looked away, thinking. She guessed that he hadn't been expecting this, and his face seemed to register that somehow it still didn't make sense.

"Jack, Sarah... you've talked to Simon, and some of the people there that night. Do you think he could have done that?"

"Honestly Tony, I don't know the man," Jack said. "Other than that one chat. But if you had asked me before this news, I would have said no. Scared, yes. Greedy? You bet. But a killer?"

"Where are they keeping Simon?" Sarah asked.

"They've moved him from Oxford to Bullingdon Prison. I doubt they'll give him bail."

"Can anyone see him?" Jack said.

Tony hesitated. "I imagine so. I've sorted out a good lawyer for him. I'll have a word."

Sarah leaned close. "And me too."

Jack smiled at that. Then: "We may learn something that, if Simon cooperates, could have us helping him... unless he really did it."

"I'll get word to his lawyer tonight and make the arrangements. I'm going to dash over to Repton Hall; see what I can do to calm Lady Repton. You know, she never seemed to care much for her grandson. But blood is blood, isn't it?"

"In this case," Jack said, "blood's also the evidence. Thanks Tony, we'll let you know how things go."

"Wonderful. And thanks to you two as well."

"SO, YOU'RE GOING to prison with me, Sarah?"

"Are you kidding? I've never been inside a real prison."

Then, a voice from behind.

"That is so *cool*, mum!"

Daniel. He loved the fact she and 'Mr. Brennan' did detective work.

Because that's what it is, thought Sarah. *Just like the TV shows he watches.*

"Cool? Guess that depends on which side of the bars you're on," Jack said.

"You've been in lots of jails, Mr. Brennan?"

Jack laughed. "Only as an observer. What is it they say on that space in Monopoly?"

"Just visiting," Daniel said.

"Right."

"Daniel, homework?"

Daniel raised a hand as if he was just about to get around to that.

"Nearly done."

"Then off you go."

He nodded, heading back to his room. And Sarah thought, not for the first time, that despite the divorce, the visits with their dad, their lives changed, Daniel and Chloe seemed to have come through it okay.

At least that's what she hoped.

"Eager to visit a jail, are we?" Jack said.

"Too right. And also ask Simon about what we've learned."

"Yes, that will be interesting. And his answers might just save his life. If…"

Jack didn't finish the thought.

"If what?"

"If we figure out what it is that's missing, what we're not seeing here."

He stood up. "When shall I pick you up?"

"Nine. At the office. Then I really need to be back by lunchtime for a call on a big new pitch we're doing. Have to make money for Chloe's trip to the Big Apple."

"See you then," he said. He started for the door. "And oh — you might want to pick yourself up a notebook as well."

12.

SIMON'S STORY

SARAH RACED OUT of her building, leaving the ever-capable Grace in charge of three big projects.

"No problem," Grace had said.

Truth is, she probably could run the place on her own!

Jack sat in his Sprite, cap and sunglasses on, as if he'd just walked out of an advert from the early sixties.

"Sorry," she said, popping into the passenger seat. "Last-minute details."

Jack smiled "That's fine. We have plenty of time. Shall I use the nice Garmin lady to get us there or—"

Sarah shook her head as Jack backed out.

"No. Just head towards Oxford, and we'll pick up the Bullingdon road on the other side. If we hit traffic on the ring road, I can get us on to some side roads."

"They're *always* fun."

She turned to Jack. She had news, and was curious how he would react.

"Jack, I got a call this morning. Early."

He turned, a nod… and she continued.

"June Rigby."

"Ah, right. The last of the hot tubbers, huh?"

"Chair of the Parish Council, I think you mean. *Very* serious woman our Ms. Rigby; there's talk of her having larger political ambitions beyond Cherringham."

"Hmm. We haven't talked to her yet. So the call?"

"Well — she gave me the rundown on the emergency meeting last night. More like a circus, apparently."

Jack gestured to a fork off. "Turn here, right?"

"Yes. So, apparently accusations were flying, some council members very unhappy discussing twinning with a murder charge in the air."

"Does sound a tad avaricious."

"But June said that Lee, Harry, and quite a few others insisted. And not only that, Marie Duval said that she was authorised to sign the deal that very night. In fact, she sounded — at least according to June — ready to pull the plug if that didn't happen."

"Interesting. Why the rush?"

"Exactly! We both know how much everyone was invested in the deal."

"So did they sign?"

"After a fair old slanging match, the council agreed to stick to the original timetable. This Friday…"

"We *really* should have gone."

Sarah laughed. "There will be minutes."

The wind blew her hair back. In just a few weeks it would be too cold for even Jack to ride around, top down. But for now, roaring through the English countryside, this was great.

"And June Rigby? Did she reveal her role in last night's 'circus'?"

"That's what's interesting. She was one of a handful who opposed moving forwards, at least for now. But they were shouted down and ultimately voted down. She stormed out."

"So — no fan of the twinning there?"

"Exactly. And not only that, she said — and it's for publication in the newsletter — she has immediately resigned her post as chair of the Parish Council."

"I thought you said she had political goals beyond Cherringham?"

"She does… or did. But for now, she said she was 'done'."

Jack grew quiet for a few moments.

Then: "Intriguing. June Rigby gone, twinning full steam ahead, even with Laurent out of the picture. Everyone on the queue… for pots of cash."

"Any thoughts? Your instincts telling you anything?"

"Yes," Jack said laughing, "they're telling me that this is one confusing case."

"Even I can see that."

"See," he said. "You're getting instincts as well."

Then, a change of subject. "Want to talk over our approach with Simon?"

Jack nodded.

Sarah reached into her purse.

"Look, I even brought a notebook."

"Now you're a real detective. So first, we need to get Simon to tell us the true story."

"Think he'll do that?"

"Murder charge hanging over him? Weapon with his prints as evidence? I think he'll be more than eager to talk."

A STOUT PRISON guard with a grim face, scowl locked in and hair in a tight bun, led them to a room with a series of small tables, each with two facing chairs.

Just like TV, Sarah thought.

Jack, though, had obviously done this before.

This *was* exciting — but it also made her nervous. Did she really belong here?

Jack seemed to sense her unease and gave her a smile. "Why don't you take the lead, hmm?" he said. "Since you know him."

"Can't say I know him that well. Tried to keep my distance, to be honest."

"You okay with that?"

She nodded. "But do drop in if I start to lose the plot."

"Got your back, as they say."

And with that, a door opened, and Simon, in a drab jumper and jeans shuffled in, eyes wide.

Slimy Simey looked very scared indeed.

SIMON SAT HUNCHED in front of them.

He looked at Jack as though expecting the detective to start asking questions.

So Sarah jumped right in.

"Simon, how're you getting on here?"

He turned to her, nodded. "All right. Not getting much sleep."

She saw Jack give her a look. Good opening question, she wondered? A bit of empathy for the accused, before bearing down?

"Has Tony arranged a lawyer for you yet?"

Simon nodded, cleared his throat. "He has someone coming down from London. Friend of his, experienced in such matters."

Jack: "But you're okay speaking to us in the meantime?"

Simon nodded. "Tony said I should. And I want this this mess to go away as fast as possible."

"So do we," Sarah said. "For you, and for your grandmother's sake. This has been very hard on her."

Sarah doubted that Simon had much concern for others considering his personality and current dire straits.

"So, ask away," he said. "This whole thing is a bloody fiasco!" He had let his voice rise, and Sarah saw the owl-eyed guard in the corner take a step forward.

Do that again, she thought, *and Simon might get scolded.*

"Okay," Sarah flipped open her notebook. "First, in your own words. What happened that night?"

"And this time, Simon, better not leave anything out," Jack added.

Another clearing of the throat.

Sarah guessed that Simon was about to 'sing'.

When your life's on the line, even the truth is worth a try.

"Okay, first thing — I didn't kill *anyone.*" He hesitated. "But I did give that fat French— um, I gave Laurent a lot of money."

"You bribed him?" Sarah said.

"Absolutely! It wasn't like everyone else *wasn't* throwing money at him. But with him all pissed and ready to blow the thing up, I gave him another grand. To sweeten his already too-sweet pot."

"But," she looked at Jack whose eyes were locked on Simon, ready to detect a lie, "you still thought he might end the deal?"

"It was on the cards. Something about the hot tub, Marie, Lee, the others. I don't know. Anyway — suddenly, twinning was the last thing he wanted to do."

Sarah nodded. "That much we knew already. So — you went after him?"

Simon hesitated. If he were to admit this, it would be crucial. Tricky thing to do, especially since his defence lawyer hadn't arrived yet.

"Yes. Found him in the bar. Tried to talk some sense into him but he wouldn't listen."

"You don't know why he went out to the island?" Jack said.

"Not a clue."

"So what happened next?"

"Bit later on, I went down to the lake. Clear the head — you know? Damned cold it was too. Saw one of the boats all the way over there, on the island…"

"So you rowed out there?" Sarah said.

Simon nodded. He took a breath.

Now she felt chilled. It was almost as if she was back there, that night. Seeing this all through Simon's eyes.

"Yeah. Got into the other boat. Pissed as well." He shook his head. "Not too bloody easy to row, after all that wine."

"You went to the island?" Sarah said, her voice low.

For a moment, she felt that she might indeed be talking to the murderer. That Simon might in fact tell them — here, now — how it happened.

"No. I mean, I wanted to. Could barely row the damn thing. But I started out, got about half way. Hit something. Banged it with my oar. Got caught in the space between the rowlock and the boat. I — I—"

Sarah and Jack said nothing.

"I reached down to give it a push. Felt something soft, then, God, must have been the wound. The body. Floating upside down."

Sarah nodded, her eyes locked on Simon.

"Somehow, I pushed the thing away. My hand… had his blood on it. Rowed like a lunatic back to the shore."

Jack shot Sarah a look.

Next question would be his.

"So — that's your story, Simon?"

13.

THE TRUTH

"IT'S NO *STORY*, I tell you! It's the bloody truth!"

The prison guard came over.

"You will keep your voice down," she said. "There will be no outbursts in the room. Understand?"

Simon nodded sheepishly, and the woman, after giving her prisoner a good long glare, went back to her corner.

"Not a story," he repeated. "That's what I did."

"Why not call the police right away?" Sarah said. "A body in the lake?"

Simon shifted in his seat.

"I could have. I mean, I thought of it. But a lot of people there that night had been, well, enjoying themselves—"

Jack leaned close, his voice low.

"You mean the coke?"

Simon nodded. "I mean, it was a big night. Maybe we all went a bit over the top. I don't know—"

"But you decided best not to have a late-night visit from the police?"

Simon hesitated. Sarah guessed he felt that he was on thin ice here. Admitting to drugs, not reporting a dead body on his property.

"Listen. I was going to call them in the morning. I mean, after I had cleaned up."

"Tossed the drugs?" Jack said.

A nod. "But I was out for the count—"

Jack again: "So your grandmother got to be the one to see that body in the lake, to call the police."

Jack did nothing to hide the disdain in his voice.

Simon became agitated, leaning close, his head swivelling from Sarah to Jack, and back again.

He may not have murdered anyone, but he sure looked guilty.

"I didn't do *anything* to Laurent. I just… panicked."

Sarah looked down at her notebook — a blank page. She was so caught up in Simon's story that she hadn't written down a thing. But now, as if for effect, she wrote down:

Tyre iron?

"What about the tyre iron?" She said. "Yours. And your prints on it."

More agitation. Simon looked as if he was about to explode, his face beetroot red.

"I didn't *know*! You hear me? That might have been mine, if it had my prints. But last time I saw it, last time I used it, it was in my car."

"So let me get this straight," said Jack. "You're saying someone went to your car and got your tyre iron because they *planned* on killing Laurent?"

Simon nodded, but then quickly backtracked.

"I suppose so. All I know is that I *don't* know how it got into that lake."

Weird as it was, with a squirming Simon in front of her, Sarah actually believed the man.

There were illegal drugs. There were bribes. Bad — horrible — decisions. He had the character of an alley cat.

But a killer?

Didn't seem likely.

Which prompted an all-important question from Sarah.

"Simon. We know it wasn't an accident. The police have the weapon, your tyre iron. So — tell us, why do you think someone would want to kill Laurent Bourdin?"

Jack looked over, a small smile on his face.

Guess I'm doing well, she thought.

Her first prison interrogation.

Simon's eyes darted left and right.

"I don't know." Then, as if by becoming louder he'd become more convincing, he raised his voice: "I don't *know!*"

The volume level made the guard storm over again.

"That will do. And time's up, anyway. Time to get this one back to his cell."

Simon's eyes looked sunken, hopeless, as the woman grabbed his right bicep and pulled him up, and out of the straight-backed wooden chair.

Then his last words.

"Please. If not for me, for my grandmother… find out who did this… why they did it."

He looked at his minder, her face stone.

She's probably heard that one a thousand times.

And Sarah and Jack watched her guide him away from the interview area.

JACK WAS STUCK behind a line of cars as the dual carriageway narrowed to one due to roadworks.

He turned to Sarah.

"Have another way around this?"

"Um, we could backtrack. But I think it would take more time than just waiting for the road crew ahead."

"Okay," he said.

When they had walked out of the jail, and driven round the Oxford ring road, Jack had been quiet, despite Sarah asking the inevitable… *what do you think?*

He had smiled as he scratched his head and said: "I'm thinking."

Now, halted by the snail's pace queue, he turned to her.

"Good work in there," he said.

"The questioning?"

"'Grilling' is what we called it, back in the day." Then: "What do you make of it all?"

"I was about to ask you the same."

"Beat you to it."

The car inched forwards a few feet.

"I believe him. Despite the evidence of the tyre iron. There was no real motive to kill Laurent. The bribe had been taken, the deal not really dead. Besides, Simon doesn't seem the murdering type."

"Agree. Problem is," Jack looked right at her, "I don't see a motive for *anyone*. Not for murder."

That made her think…

Not for murder.

"Hang on. You mean, there's a motive for—"

"Dunno. If the deal was going south, people could try bigger bribes, more money. Angry, yes. But enough to kill? Doubtful."

Another few feet.

There were going nowhere fast but that was okay. It was a good time to review where they were.

"Of course," Jack said slowly as if the idea just came to him, "the Council chair, June Rigby. She doesn't sound like a fan of the twinning." He took a breath. "Maybe because it wasn't her idea?"

"She was always behind it. But something must have made her change her mind."

By this point they were only feet away from a road worker with a bright orange vest holding a paddle-shaped sign that alternated from "stop" to "go".

Jack kept looking ahead. Then, a slap to the steering wheel.

An 'ah-ha' moment.

"All right. Now I'm convinced."

Sarah could barely wait for where Jack's instincts and training were about to bring him.

"We're missing something big. And it has to do with that island. Been bothering me for a while now. One boat goes over. Laurent's killed on the island. But if Simon is telling the truth and he never got as far as the island… Then who did? And how did they get there? The key to this is the island, the temple."

Sarah saw where this was leading.

"The police have Simon dead to rights, unless we find something. And if I'm right — about missing pieces, about the island — then I'm afraid there's one person we need speak to again."

And suddenly Sarah knew exactly who.

"Lady Repton?"

"Exactly. Hate to bother the old gal, but if anyone knows that place, it's her. Besides, she's got a pretty quick and shrewd mind herself."

Sarah laughed at that.

"That's for sure."

The sign in front of them twirled round, signalling that they could move off, and finally they were driving again.

"Want to give Tony a call? See if we can meet her this afternoon? After your conference call at the office, of course. But better sooner than later. I'm afraid time's not on our side — or Simon's either."

And beyond the roadworks at last, Jack's Sprite finally picked up speed as they headed back to Cherringham.

14.

SECRETS OF THE HALL

JACK STOOD BY the side of the lake and peered at the island through the murky afternoon gloom.

"In the summer of course, it comes into its own," said Lady Repton who stood at his side. "When I was a child we had garden parties down here. A string quartet would set up in front of the temple. They'd play long into the evening. There were lights in all the trees."

"Must have been quite magical," said Jack.

"Just memories now. And sadly no one left to share them with."

"Does anyone go out to the island these days?"

"Only the gardeners. They have to cut the grass by hand. Awful job, you know."

"I can imagine. Guess they use one of these?"

Jack pointed towards the two little rowing boats tied up to the jetty: he could see tattered stubs of police tape still fluttering from the railings.

"That's right."

"And there's no other way out to the island?"

"No, these are the only boats."

"Is it swimmable?"

"Looks harmless, doesn't it?" said Lady Repton. "But the water's treacherous, especially at night. And especially — I imagine — after drinking all that wine! Mud, reeds, rocks — even as children we knew never to swim in there."

Jack nodded. He could see the mist thickening over the lake. He shivered involuntarily and pulled his jacket tight.

"You should get back inside," he said.

"You're right. This is no day to catch a chill."

"Maybe you could tell Sarah I'll be another hour or so? I think she's up in the house somewhere working…"

"Of course."

"Meanwhile, if you don't mind, I'd like to take one of the boats and check out the island."

"Be my guest," said Lady Repton. "As I said the other day, you have free run of the estate. My grandson is an idiot of the highest order, but I know he is innocent and I will not have him languishing in prison. In Bullingdon too of all places! Bullingdon! God forbid!"

Jack watched as she turned and headed back up the grassy slope towards the house, which was fast disappearing in the mist.

He walked down the jetty and climbed into one of the rowboats. He slotted the oars into place then untied the mooring rope and pushed away.

Seconds later he was rowing out towards the island.

What was that film?

No, it was a TV series, he and Katherine had watched on HBO. *Brideshead Revisited.*

If she could see me now, thought Jack. *Rowing across an ornamental lake to my own private Grecian Temple.*

To the Manor Born…

It only took a minute to reach the island — but threading the boat through the rocks which jutted out from the dark water's edge took longer. Eventually Jack found the way through, and stepping out of the boat on to the grass, he looped the rope around a rock to secure it.

He looked around.

The island was no more than a hundred yards across. Meadow grass at the edges and then, in its centre, a dark wood of oak and chestnut trees, thick with ivy.

The temple was just as imposing out here as it was viewed from the house. Built of white marble, it had a high porch suspended on four classical pillars: behind the pillars a tall heavy door stood just open.

Jack turned and looked back at the house.

From here even at night you'd clearly be able to see figures approaching the far jetty. And while they rowed across, they'd have their back to you.

Easy enough to ambush an unsuspecting visitor.

And the woods provided perfect cover. Wait till they were tying up — then *wallop!*

He approached the temple door and pushed it open, then backed away fast as a pigeon fluttered and flapped in panic against his face before flying away.

The police had left the door open — who knew what wildlife would now make this their home?

He turned around. The temple was bare, apart from some bird droppings. White walls and tall windows with recessed stone benches beneath. A stone floor. A tall cupola. A set of steps with a railing that curled up to an open gallery and window.

Otherwise… nothing.

What had he expected? Cops had been out here for a day, they'd have taken away any evidence — if there'd been any.

It wasn't even certain that the temple was connected anyway. The murder weapon had been found out here, but the killer — whoever it was — might just have waited down in those woods, in the darkness, ready to pounce…

But even the best cops miss stuff — he knew that from personal experience. And if they were going to get Simon off the hook, they were going to need evidence.

He climbed the steps which led up to the cupola. At the top there was a small balcony — room enough to sit — and a window that looked out upon the lake.

Jack peered out — he could see the little jetty at the edge of the lake, and behind it the Hall itself. And by pressing himself back against the stone wall he figured he was probably invisible to anybody down in the temple below.

Good place to keep watch, he thought.

Then he climbed down the stairs, went over to one of the stone seats and sat.

In his mind's eye he turned the room into grids, then square-by-square he stared at each one, searching for clues.

Exactly as he'd been taught to do when he was a rookie detective.

Don't think — just look.

After half an hour, he'd done the walls and the windows. He reached into his pocket and treated himself to a mint.

Now the floor.

It was solid flagstones in rows.

He counted the rows. Fifteen up, twelve across. One hundred and eighty squares.

He squatted down in one corner and started checking each stone carefully on his hands and knees. Looking for signs, marks, recent scratches, running his finger round the mortared edges…

Gotta get my knees looked at, he thought, as he shuffled awkwardly from one stone to the next. *This had better be worth it.*

HALF WAY THROUGH the task he stopped dead. One of the heavy stones was different from the others: twice the width, but it had a mortar line edged across it. Good enough to pass a casual inspection — it fit the size and pattern of the other stones perfectly.

But as he ran his finger round the edge he could feel that the mortar was actually a lip of stone, a clever disguise.

It wasn't mortar at all.

Jack got up quickly –

Ouch, too quickly —

– and went out to the boat. He pulled one of the heavy metal oarlocks out of its socket, grabbed an oar too, and went back into the temple. Kneeling down, he tapped a nearby stone with the oarlock. It gave a heavy, muted sound.

Then he tapped the stone in question. It echoed. There was some kind of empty space beneath it. The oarlock had a sharp end — he'd remembered correctly.

He slipped the point into the tiny gap between this stone and the next, and slid the oar under it to make a fulcrum.

Then he placed his boot on the oarlock and pressed down with all his weight. The oarlock pivoted on the oar... and the stone lifted a couple of inches. While it was up, he quickly slid the oar round to wedge it open, then stepped back.

Then, squatting carefully he gripped the edge of the stone, lifted it up and laid it on its side.

In the fading light one thing was clear: the underneath of the stone slab was scored and marked with fresh scratches.

And he hadn't made them.

Somebody recently had moved this stone.

Now Jack turned his attention to the oblong manhole, which the slab had concealed. He peered down into the dark hole — but it was impossible to tell how deep it was.

He took out his cell phone, checked the battery and flicked it into torch mode. Pointing it at the hole he could see an old, rusted set of metal hoops leading down — and he could just see a stone floor about twenty feet below.

Well whaddya know — a secret tunnel just itching to be explored.

And with excitement building like he was a kid again, he put the phone between his teeth, swung himself round and climbed down the ladder into the darkness...

15.

AFTERNOON TEA

SARAH CHECKED THE time on her laptop. It was nearly five — and already it was getting dark outside.

Where was Jack?

Lady Repton had installed her here in the old kitchen a couple of hours ago — "warmest room in the house my dear and apparently a serviceable Wi-Fi signal — isn't that what you youngsters want all the time?"

Long while since anyone called me a youngster, thought Sarah.

She'd spent the time with her laptop on the big old kitchen table, going through various statements which Tony had emailed her, forwarded from Simon's new and extremely expensive defence lawyer.

From those statements and the interviews she and Jack had made, she'd managed to draw up a flow-chart showing everyone's locations on the night of the murder.

Now, she needed Jack here to go through them before she had to dash off to sort out the kids.

She checked her phone for texts.

Hmm, not like him to be out of contact, she thought.

And, for the first time, she felt anxious about his safety. If they were right, there was a murderer still at large.

She shivered — in spite of the warmth of the old kitchen. Lady Repton was right — this place, with its giant gas range and ancient radiators was indeed warm and cosy in spite of its size.

Once upon a time this kitchen had been tasked with preparing dinners by the score.

But the old cook who'd clocked off at four-thirty (leaving Lady Repton's supper to be microwaved when she wanted) had told her that the conference centre was serviced by a new set of kitchens in the extension.

This place was now run solely for family.

Just Lady Repton and Simon. And tonight he'd be dining with his new friends in Bullingdon Prison…

Once there'd been a staff of fifty here full-time, the cook had said: now there was just her, a couple of part-time maids and the gardeners.

And after they left, the place was empty. Not a soul, apart from Lady Repton.

Sarah started to pack away her laptop. She was going to have to find Jack herself — or order a taxi back to Cherringham.

She reached for her coat –

– which was when she heard the sound…

A rattling, echoing deep within the house below.

Below? What was down there? Cellars?

Sarah felt a pang of fear.

Ridiculous, she thought. *Must be one of the staff, still here.*

But no — the cook had said they all got a lift home together.

So it must be Lady Repton.

But Lady Repton wouldn't be venturing down to the cellars, especially after dark, when the staff had gone home.

The rattling started again — now more frenetic.

And was that a voice — shouting?

Sarah's mind raced: what if there was someone else who lived in the house, someone they'd all failed to record in their notes and interviews?

Not Simon, not one of the hot tubbers.

But somebody unknown.

Unknown and dangerous.

The real killer!

The idea seemed crazy.

The rattling continued.

No, this was ridiculous.

She was going to have to confront this sound, ignore her fears.

She crossed the empty kitchen, tracking towards the noise. In the far corner was a door.

She opened it. Stairs down into darkness: she reached around for a light switch, found it and flicked it on.

It's the cellars.

Swallowing hard, she stepped forwards, down the cold stone cellar steps.

The rattling grew louder.

At the bottom of the steps she looked round. The cellar was enormous, as if it might stretch underneath the whole house.

Racks and racks of ancient pots and pans, old tins, dusty boxes.

A dank, musty smell.

Bare stone floor and cobwebs everywhere.

This place clearly wasn't used much anymore. Perhaps only by Simon to retrieve his wine, she thought, because there along one wall stood racks with hundreds of bottles.

Bare light bulbs hung from the ceiling, illuminating the cellar as far as Sarah could see.

The rattling came again, then a *bang, bang, bang* — as if someone were trying to smash a door down.

She walked down the aisle towards the sound, making her way between racks of old boxes until she came to a wall with a tall empty cupboard.

The banging was coming from behind the cupboard.

And the cupboard was jolting and moving with each thump.

What am I doing? I must be crazy, thought Sarah, surprising herself with her own bravery. *I wouldn't have done this a year ago...*

She reached out to the cupboard and pulled it back.

Surprisingly, it slid back easily.

She saw a door behind the cupboard, with a heavy bolt drawn across it.

She took a deep breath, and slid back the bolt.

Then turned the door handle and pulled the door wide open.

A bright light blinded her and she stepped back.

Then the light switched off — and she could see…

Jack! Standing in the doorway grinning at her.

"Well, hey there partner. What kept you?"

JACK CHUCKED A couple of logs into the little wood-burner then shut the glass door with the poker.

"There you go, boy," said Jack to his dog.

Riley looked up at him as if to check there were going to be no more disturbances, then lay down again on his cushion in front of the fire.

Jack picked up his mug of tea again and sat back in his armchair opposite Sarah.

Good to be back on the Grey Goose on a night like this, he thought.

"You've got the place nice and snug," said Sarah from the sofa.

"Last winter was pretty cold — I'm figuring with this little stove — if we get another bad one — I can stay warm and cook too."

"It can happen. The winds we get up here push the snowdrifts — only three roads in and out and we're easily cut off from the world," said Sarah. "It'll be a couple of months away yet though."

Jack sat back feeling pretty content, all things considered. Sarah was good company and — with the breakthrough in the case back on the island — he had that old thrill of being back in the game again.

Not that the case was solved.

But he felt it was accelerating towards a conclusion. Funny how investigations picked up momentum…

"One thing I still don't quite get," said Sarah. "Why didn't the police find the trapdoor out at the temple? They had a couple of days to search the place."

"They weren't looking for it," said Jack. "They had Simon in the frame. Their scenario required two boats — and they found two boats."

"So it was… illogical to search for another way on to the island?"

"Spot on. Illogical — unless you believed somebody else was out there that night."

"Okay. What happens now?" said Sarah.

"Good question. We know it was possible for somebody to get to the island unseen — we just don't know who."

"Or why," said Sarah. "Show me the note again."

Jack took the small clear sandwich bag out of his pocket and laid it on the coffee table between them.

"Exhibit number one, your honour," said Jack. "The crumpled note found by the detective in the tunnel under the lake."

He watched as Sarah picked it up and examined it again closely under the reading light by the sofa.

"'It's a deal. Take a boat. Meet me on the island tonight'," said Sarah, reading aloud from the slip of paper. "How do we know it's not years old? Maybe it was lying in the water at the bottom of that tunnel since Victorian times?"

"I thought that too," said Jack. "But if you look carefully you can see the little logo — Repton Hall Conference Centre. The water almost washed it out — but not quite."

"So it can't be more than a month or two old."

"Exactly," said Jack. "Crumpled up, dropped by mistake — another few days it would have been gone. Just a soggy mess."

He watched Sarah thinking.

"You know, Jack, it doesn't *seem* to say much, but in fact it does say quite a lot."

"Go on."

"First — 'it's a deal'. There's been a conversation, an argument, a proposition. And recent enough that the writer knows that Laurent will understand what 'deal' refers to—"

"You're assuming it was written for Laurent?"

"We have to, don't we? This note's the only motive we have for him going out to the island."

"Okay, I'll go with that."

"Good. Second — 'take a boat'. Either the writer didn't know about the tunnel, or they didn't want to give away its existence. And third — 'meet me'. Me — not us. It's a one-to-one arrangement."

"Sounds like there's a fourth?"

"Well, yes. It's kind of obvious — but 'island' locates the message to Repton Hall. It's not a note written about a meeting at a different location — say in the village. No, it's about that *island* — on that night."

"You're right. Good thinking."

"Learning from the best. Only trouble is — we still don't have a prime suspect," said Sarah. "It could be anybody."

"It's one of the hot tubbers though — don't you think?"

Sarah laughed. "I do," she said. "That's what my instinct says. I just can't back it up."

"Welcome to the police force," said Jack laughing too.

"It makes sense though, doesn't it? They were going to profit from the twinning. So when Laurent said he wanted to pull out of the deal…"

"Laurent had to go," said Jack. "And we know — thanks to you — that Marie can't wait to sign. Only trouble is, they're all backing each other up."

"If you were back on the force, what would you do now?"

"Easy. I'd bring 'em all in, one at a time and keep asking questions till one broke down."

"But we can't do that," said Sarah.

"Nope," said Jack. "One of the downsides of being an amateur detective."

"There are some advantages, though, Jack."

Jack stared at her. He'd seen that playful look on her face before.

"Okay…" he said. "Exactly which law are you thinking of breaking, Sarah?"

She shrugged innocently. Jack had seen that innocent shrug before, too.

"Not *breaking* a law, exactly," she said. "More like… bending it a little?"

"Go on."

"You got anything planned for tomorrow night?"

"Sounds like maybe I don't…"

"Good. Because we're going fishing."

"Let me guess — not for trout?"

"No, not trout. Truth," said Sarah, shaking her head with a smile.

He listened as she set about explaining her plan.

16.

ENTENTE NOT SO CORDIALE

"YOU KNOW, WE weren't really planning on having dinner, Lady Repton," said Jack, his arms filled with the ancient picnic basket.

"Nonsense, dear boy," said Lady Repton, now handing a pile of chequered blankets to Sarah. "You may well be out there all night. So I had Cook make up two flasks of Mulligatawny and you'll find a very serviceable cheddar in one of the tins."

Jack stowed the basket under the seat of his little fibreglass dinghy and took one last look around the lake in the fading light.

"We really have to get going, Sarah," he said.

"Don't let me hold you up," said Lady Repton.

"You will stay inside, Lady Repton, won't you?" said Sarah, as she climbed carefully into the little boat. "Seriously. This really might be dangerous."

"Don't worry about me," said Lady Repton. "I'm not much use in a fight anymore. But give me a shout on the walkie-talkie and I'll have the police here in two shakes."

Jack climbed onto the boat and grabbed hold of the oars, as Lady Repton cast off and gave them a gentle push into the dark waters of the lake.

"Isn't this exciting!" she said as they drifted away from the jetty with its two moored wooden boats, and Jack began to row.

He watched as Lady Repton gave them a brief wave then turned and walked quickly back to the house.

"No use in a fight — anymore," said Sarah. "You hear that?"

"I did indeed," said Jack. "There's more to that old lady than meets the eye." Then: "Glad we're helping her with this."

He rowed a few more strokes, and peering over his shoulder he could see the island drawing near.

"What the hell's Mulligatawny by the way?"

"Curry soup," said Sarah. "Relic of our imperial past."

"You don't say. Well, I guess if it was good enough for the redcoats, it'll do me just fine. It's going to be pretty cold out here."

He looked down at the boat, checking they'd brought everything. Didn't want to be out on the island missing something vital. Because this plan was based on a lot of 'ifs' and 'maybes'…

First of all — would all the hot tubbers have received Sarah's spoof email?

It hadn't taken her long to find the addresses for everyone who'd been at the fateful twinning dinner. After excluding the likes of Tony and Cecil — and those who had a strong alibi — they'd decided on just five names: Harry and Vanessa, June, Lee and Marie.

Sarah had shown him what the mail would look like when it came: no headers, no apparent coding, no clue as to the sender, simply the words 'A Friend' in the sender's tab.

And within the mail the message which was intended to set a chill in the killer's heart — whoever they were: *'Meet me on the island at midnight — or the police get to hear all about what you were up to on Saturday night'.*

In theory, it was a good tactic. But what if the killer wasn't one of those five? What if they never got the mail? And worse — what if they did turn up — but ready to kill again?

Lady Repton had listened to the plan carefully — and suggested she should have a role too, as lookout. Hence the walkie-talkie. In truth, Jack had been grateful. It was good to know there was someone they could contact if things did get out of hand.

He hoped they wouldn't.

Guess we'll know soon enough, thought Jack.

The little boat bumped against the rocks of the island.

"We're here," said Sarah, disturbing his thoughts.

Jack paddled through the jagged stones until the boat rested against the grassy bank. Then he climbed out and tied up. Sarah handed him the blankets and the picnic basket, plus his old duffel bag and jacket.

"Let's get the boat hidden in the trees," he said.

Unlike the Repton rowing boats back at the jetty, Jack's dinghy - which they'd brought on the back of Sarah's Rav-4 - was light enough to carry.

In a matter of minutes, they'd hidden the boat in the undergrowth and were standing between the pillars of the old temple.

Jack took out his old flashlight and switched it on, then beckoned to Sarah to follow him into the temple. When they were inside, he pushed the door to.

"Yikes. This place is pretty spooky," said Sarah. "Where are we going to hide?"

Jack trained the light on the steps. "The perfect lookout point."

He led the way to the balcony, then laid out the blankets, food basket and duffel.

"Check out the view," said Jack, nodding to the window.

Jack leaned against the glass with Sarah and peered out: already it was so dark that the far edge of the lake was hardly visible. Half a mile away across the sloping lawns, he could just see the outline of Repton Hall.

He saw a light in one of the upstairs windows and a figure moving. He pulled out a small walkie-talkie from his pocket and spoke into it:

"Jack to hall, Jack to hall. You reading me?"

"Reading you loud and clear Jack. This is hall, over."

He shook his head and grinned at that.

"You might want to turn the light off now, ma'am."

"Wilco!"

Jack turned to Sarah who stood next to him, and mouthed — 'wilco'?

She shrugged and grinned back.

"Radio silence until you see something, over."

"Understood, Jack. Over and out."

Jack clicked off the walkie-talkie, then turned to Sarah:

"You know, if you offered her the chance to do this again, and the only downside was that her grandson had to stay in prison for a week — I think she'd jump at the offer."

"If Simon was your grandson, wouldn't you?"

"Yeah, maybe," said Jack grinning at her.

He watched as Sarah sat down on the blanket.

"And we might as well eat while there's still some light," she said.

"Sure," said Jack, joining her and putting his flashlight down. "Our guests might decide to come early…"

SARAH WOKE SUDDENLY with a jolt, completely confused, not sure where she was.

Then she saw Jack, standing above her, his face lit by moonlight through the temple window.

"We got visitors," he said softly.

She scrambled quickly to her feet and joined him at the window.

"Where?" she said, raising her eyes above the windowsill and looking out across the lake.

"Somewhere down by the jetty —"

The walkie-talkie in Jack's hand crackled.

"On one of the boats now," came Lady Repton's voice on low volume.

"Who is it?" said Jack into the walkie-talkie.

"Can't tell," said Lady Repton. "Too dark. Over."

"Okay," said Jack. "Radio silence for now please, Lady Repton. You know what to do if I call again."

"Wilco, Temple. Roger and out."

Sarah peered into the darkness. She could see the boat moving towards them, oars splashing on the moonlit water.

"Any idea who it is?" said Sarah.

"Nope," said Jack. "I know one thing though — rowing like

that they're going to be lucky to make it without drowning."

"This is going to be interesting," said Sarah.

"That's for sure. Just need to let them make the moves."

Sarah could just see Jack's face in the darkness. He was smiling. And she realised — a year ago, maybe, she would have been worried. But now, knowing Jack as she did — she felt confident.

If he wasn't worried — then she shouldn't be.

But then she also remembered — when he truly *was* worried, he was also pretty good at hiding it…

"How long was I asleep?" she said.

"Half an hour, maybe."

"Sorry, Jack."

"Hey, no problem. You got kids and a job — gotta grab the sleep when you can."

Hmm, she thought, *I do have kids and a job. So what am I doing out here on an island getting ready to ambush a killer —*

But there wasn't more time to think, because down in the temple she could hear the main door creaking open and she now saw the beam of a torch cutting into the darkness below.

She crept forward on the balcony, her body low, so she could see over the rim of stone.

Just who was it, who'd sneaked on to the estate, taken a rowing boat and come out to the island in the middle of the night…?

Was it the killer?

She was about to find out …

17.

MET BY MOONLIGHT

THROUGH THE OLD iron bars of the balcony railing, Sarah saw a tall figure standing in the middle of the temple. She recognised the shape instantly.

It was Vanessa Howden!

Sarah looked at Jack who was now lying next to her. He shrugged — he could clearly see the turkey-farmer's wife too and seemed just as surprised.

But then another torch clicked on — and Sarah realised that two people had come across on the boat.

There was no mistaking the other figure either — Cherringham's one-time chair of the Parish Council: June Rigby.

A torch beam slid up the steps towards the balcony where Sarah and Jack were lying. She pulled back quickly away from the light.

"See anything?" said Vanessa, her voice booming.

"For God's sake, do keep it *down*," said June.

"Don't be pathetic, June. There's clearly nobody here."

"So what do we do now?" said June.

"We wait."

"This is ridiculous. Total waste of time. Nobody's going to turn up—"

"Oh really? Listen! What's that then? The ghost of Laurent Bourdin?"

"Vanessa, do you have no feelings at all?"

From outside the temple, Sarah heard the bang of another boat hitting the rocks at the edge of the island, followed by a muffled curse, splashing and more cursing.

While she and Jack had been concentrating on the happy couple below, somebody else had clearly taken the other boat and rowed to the island.

The arrival of a third hot tubber was now causing chaos in the temple. She saw one of the torches turn off.

"Turn your bloody torch off," said Vanessa.

"No!" said June. "Turn yours on! I don't want to be out here in the dark with some blackmailer on the loose…"

"Always have to be in charge, don't you," said Vanessa. "Do you never give up telling people what to do?"

"Pot and kettle, Vanessa, pot and kettle…"

Sarah watched as Vanessa's torch flicked back on.

Jack leaned in close to Sarah: "Any guesses on who the new arrival is?" he whispered.

"Right now, I have no idea," said Sarah.

"Join the club," said Jack with a baffled shake of his head. "But you gotta admit; this sure is worth the entry fee."

Sarah slid forward to the edge of the balcony and gazed down at the door to the temple. The two women had both now trained their torches on the door.

Who else had read her email and had something to hide? Who was the mysterious third guest to the island?

She watched as the door creaked open and a man stepped into the temple holding his own torch, its beam now lighting up the two startled women…

"Harry!" said Vanessa. "What the *hell* are you doing here?"

"Vanessa?" said Harry Howden. "I thought you were at book club?"

"And you — you're supposed to be in Chipping Norton meeting suppliers!"

Sarah watched as Harry's torch flicked sideways and lit up June's face.

"You're blinding me, you idiot, put it away," said June.

"Well if it isn't our helpful ex-chair," said Harry.

"What are you doing here?" said June.

"You sent me an email telling me to come," said Harry. "Didn't you?"

"No, I didn't," said June.

"Well, somebody did," said Harry. "And I assume it wasn't you, Vanessa."

"Don't be ridiculous," said Vanessa. "I don't need to know what you were up to on Saturday night. Because to my eternal shame, I do already. Cavorting like a damned teenager. Champagne! Drugs! Girls! You should be ashamed of yourself. If my friends in Cherringham knew—"

"All right, all right, we've been through it a million times, let's just forget it shall we?" said Harry, with what sounded to Sarah like despair.

Sarah watched as he stared glumly at the two women.

"So then — who did send the email?" he said. "And why did he send it to you two?"

Vanessa and Jane looked nervously at each other.

Very shifty, thought Sarah.

"I don't know," said June.

"I can't… imagine," said Vanessa.

"Oh yeah?" said Harry. "Don't forget — we're all in this together. And when his lordship goes to court we need to be telling the same story. Or you won't *have* any friends left in Cherringham."

Sarah looked at Jack, next to her. Were they going to get a confession? Jack winked and held up his walkie-talkie.

"Lady R is getting the whole deal on that little recorder I gave her," he whispered.

"Priceless," said Sarah.

"All right," said June. "Let's just say… we are slightly involved."

"Not intentionally," said Vanessa. "Things just… got out of control."

"Go on," said Harry. "I want to hear this."

"That night," said June. "In the hot tub. I suddenly realised what was really going on. How corrupt the whole twinning project had become."

"Corrupt?" said Harry. "It was just business. It's how the real world works, June, how the wheels get oiled—"

"Drugs? Bribery? Kickbacks?" said June. "That's not 'just business'. Or if it is — I want no part of it."

"So what happened?" said Harry. "You obviously did something else that night that you're ashamed of. What?"

She hesitated. Sarah was afraid June Rigby might — as they say — 'clam up'. But after a moment, she continued. "After you and Simon agreed to pay Laurent the extra he was demanding—"

"How do you know about that?" said Harry.

"I followed you to the bar," said June. "Overheard you."

"So much for your moral high ground. You *spied* on us."

"Whatever. Anyway — that's when I decided I'd had enough. So I didn't go back to the tub. I just… went up to bed—"

"Which is where I met her — on the landing," said Vanessa.

"What were *you* doing there?" said Harry.

"I was on my way to drag you away from that bloody hot tub, what do you think?" said Vanessa.

"Oh, right."

"Vanessa told me she wanted to kill the whole deal too," said June. "She also said she'd looked out of the window and seen Lee and Marie on the island, together, you know, doing…"

"We knew Laurent and Marie were an item," said Vanessa. "So we wrote a note telling him if he went out to the island he'd get his cash…"

"I slid it under his door…" said June.

"And twenty minutes later, I saw him rowing out there," said Vanessa. "I knew if he spotted Lee with Marie, he'd stop the twinning."

"And destroy my bloody business with it," said Harry. "Didn't you care — about us?"

"I care about you, Harry," said Vanessa. "It was for your own good. You and France would have destroyed us!"

"What happened then?" said Harry. "Don't tell me you killed

him, June?"

"You are so stupid…" said June. "Do I look like a killer?"

"How would I know?" said Harry. "But if you didn't kill him — was it Simon after all?"

"No, he was in no state to do anything," said June. "I went back to the hot tub to make sure he was okay. He was still there, all on his own. Sad, really. I managed to get him to his room — and that was the last I saw of him."

"So if none of us killed Laurent…" said Harry. "Then who did?"

From deep below the temple, Sarah heard a loud clang — the sound of metal against stone.

At the same instant, next to her, Jack stood up and switched on his light, pointing it down at the shocked and surprised faces of the three guilty hot tubbers.

"Evening, folks. I think we're all about to find out the answer to that question," said Jack.

"What the hell — Brennan?" said Harry, pointing his torch up at Sarah and Jack. "What's going on?"

Sarah watched as Jack started down the steps, keeping his light on Vanessa, Harry and June as he went.

"Best do as I say," he continued. "Somebody's coming. And we'll all be just fine. That okay with everybody?"

Sarah took the steps behind him.

The killer was on the way — and she wanted to be right next to Jack when they arrived.

JACK LEANED AGAINST the wall and figured how it was going to play out.

Because now he knew who he was dealing with, he had a plan.

Funny — right from the beginning they'd been thinking the motive was all about the twinning.

Whereas in reality, it was that old, old story. A man and a woman. And another man…

From beneath his feet there now came the sound of metal on

stone. A scraping and levering sound. Grunts, the sound of physical exertion.

"Everybody ready?" he said quietly into the pitch darkness inside the temple. The moon had gone in and the place was totally black.

He'd gotten them all to turn off their flashlights — not because it was strictly necessary, but it would just be a more dramatic surprise to this latest entry in the 'where were you that night?' contest.

And what better setting for the big reveal than an old temple on an island in the middle of an English country estate?

Certainly beat some dealer's den on a wet night in the projects…

The clanging sound got louder, and then Jack saw a glimmer of light from the cracks in the stone floor. The slice of light expanded as a whole stone slab lifted slowly in the air, towards Jack and the others who stood next to him.

Jack had made them stand this side so that whoever emerged from the tunnel would only be able to see them once the stone had been completely pushed back.

He looked at Sarah — he could tell she was enjoying this too. Then he turned back to watch as a head then shoulders now popped up, silhouetted against the broad beam of light from the flashlight they carried.

The figure swept the torch around the temple, and just as it swung round towards Jack:

"Now," he said, switching on his own flashlight.

With perfect timing the others turned on their lights too — and the five beams converged on the face of Lee Jones.

"Aagh, what the—" he said. "Turn those bloody things off, will you, I can't see!"

"Lee!" said voices at Jack's side as the identity of their surprise guest was revealed.

"Sorry, Lee," said Jack. "But I think we'll keep them on, if you don't mind."

"What's going on?" said Lee.

"I think you're about to be arrested for murder," said Sarah. "Or at the very least, manslaughter."

"Bollocks," said Lee. "You can't prove anything."

Jack played his own flashlight down towards Lee's hand.

"Is that a tyre iron I see before me?" said Jack.

"What?"

"I guess this time you had to bring one with you from your own car. Couldn't pinch one from Simon's — since the police have that one as evidence already."

"I don't know what the hell you're talking about," said Lee. "Harry, June — what's this all about?"

"Might as well come clean, Lee," said Harry. "When the game's up, you can't fight it. I should know…"

Jack stared at Lee: he was clearly making his mind up.

"See if I can't," said Lee.

And Jack watched as the car salesman swung round and down into the tunnel to make his escape. He landed with a loud splash, and they all heard him deep below as his echoing footsteps faded into the distance, running back towards the Hall.

"Shouldn't we try and stop him?" said June.

"By the time he reaches the house, the police will be waiting for him," said Jack, holding up the walkie-talkie. "Isn't that right, Lady Repton?"

"They're here already, Jack," came Lady Repton's voice from the walkie-talkie. "As you cops say — we've got him bang to rights I do believe."

18.

A LITTLE R & R

SARAH SIPPED AT her champagne as she sat back in the hot tub, the bubbles flowing around her neck.

"I suppose back in the day when you were with the NYPD, you ended every case like this," she said.

"Sure," said Jack, who was sitting opposite her. "We had a hot tub in the precinct house. Some days we never left it. Fridge stocked with champagne as well!"

She laughed, and then looked across through the glass wall into the leisure centre.

Daniel and Chloe were enjoying having the whole pool to themselves, throwing a giant inflatable back and forth.

"Funny," she said. "The only time they'll still play is when they're in the sea or in a pool. Rest of the time they wouldn't be seen dead together."

"Growing up fast," said Jack, sipping his own champagne, before carefully placing the flute at the side of the hot tub.

"You should get your daughter over here, Jack," said Sarah. "Hey, tell her you belong to the country club now. Along with Lady Repton, the club members are the nearest thing to aristocracy we have in Cherringham."

"It's a year's free membership — and one year only, remember? The Reptons are grateful, but they're not going to break the bank to say thank you."

"You just keep reminding Simon about his week in prison,

and he won't forget," said Sarah.

"He's lucky we were here to help, I gotta admit. And lucky that he has such a great grandmother."

"Do you think Lee and Marie would have got away with it?" said Sarah.

"I don't see any of that lot sacrificing their success voluntarily to keep Simon out of jail — do you?"

"Too much to lose," said Sarah. "Though I'd like to believe June would have come clean."

"Maybe."

"You think Marie was going to leave Lee to carry the can?"

"Looks like it," said Jack. "Don't forget — she was going to have to own up not just to one affair, but to two. Laurent *and* Lee. And I know the French are pretty liberal about these things, but even they might complain a little about that…"

"I don't think they'll charge her though," said Sarah. "She says Laurent attacked her first — and I saw the evidence. Very nasty marks on her neck and face too, hence the sunglasses she refused to take off."

"Lee's got a pretty good defence too — *sauvez la femme*, isn't that what they say?"

"If it really did play out like that."

"Exactly," said Jack. "If. Guess we'll never know."

The bubbles subsided.

"Want some more?" said Sarah.

"You bet," said Jack.

Sarah hit the button and the bubble action started again.

"You know, right at the beginning, if we'd looked at the old staff photos in the corridor there, we'd have found a young Lee Jones. He's in both 1988 and 1989, smiling at the camera with his arm round a kitchen maid."

"Every case — you can look back and see a short cut," said Jack. "But we were following the money, Sarah. We wouldn't have connected Lover-boy Lee to the island. And the girls he took out there — we would have just thought he used the boats…"

"You're right," said Sarah. "He wasn't going to own up to knowing about the tunnel until the game was up."

"Any more news on the twinning?"

"Not a whisper," said Sarah. "And apparently the item has been quietly deleted from the agenda for the next Parish Council meeting."

"How very Cherringham," said Jack with a smile.

The door to the hot tub area opened up and Sarah saw Simon peering in.

"Can I get you chaps anything?" he said. "Open tab all day, you know."

"We're fine thanks, Simon," said Sarah.

"Jolly good," said Simon. "Dinner for four at your usual table?"

"You bet," said Jack. "Though Simon perhaps you could have a word with chef for me?"

"Of course, Jack," said Simon. "I hope there isn't a problem…"

"No, no," said Jack. "It's just I'm aiming to have the oysters tonight, and if chef doesn't mind, I'd quite like to make my own sauce."

"Not a problem. I'll make sure he's ready."

Sarah watched Simon go then turned to Jack.

"Well, you're certainly making yourself at home," she said.

Jack smiled at her.

"I'm retired," he said. "A guy's got to do something with all the hours in the day."

He raised his glass.

"To a life of leisure," said Jack.

"I wish," said Sarah.

NEXT IN THE SERIES:

CHERRINGHAM
A COSY CRIME SERIES

SNOWBLIND

Matthew Costello & Neil Richards

One of the worst blizzards in years hits Cherringham, cutting off the village from the rest of the world. Just outside of town, Broadmead Grange is a struggling retirement home, housed in a gothic mansion behind towering walls.

One of the home's residents, poor old Archy, becomes Cherringham's latest victim after he loses himself amongst the snow drifts.

Did Archy really just fall victim to the elements, or was there foul play involved?

Jack and Sarah take on the case to dig up the truth.

ABOUT THE AUTHORS

Matthew Costello (US-based) and **Neil Richards** (UK) have been writing TV scripts together for more than twenty years. The best-selling Cherringham series is their first collaboration as fiction writers: since its first publication as ebooks and audiobooks the series has sold over a million copies.

Matthew is the author of many successful novels, including *Vacation* (2011), *Home* (2014) and *Beneath Still Waters* (1989), which was adapted by Lionsgate as a major motion picture. He has written for The Disney Channel, BBC, SyFy and has also written dozens of bestselling games including the critically acclaimed *The 7th Guest*, *Doom 3*, *Rage* and *Pirates of the Caribbean*.

Neil has worked as a producer and writer in TV and film, creating scripts for BBC, Disney, and Channel 4, and earning numerous Bafta nominations along the way. He's also written script and story for over 20 video games including *The Da Vinci Code* and *Broken Sword*.

Printed in Great Britain
by Amazon